S0-AAB-130

EAST JUSTICE

by
Melanie Braverman

*For Candy,
who loves who I love
and thank-you for it all.
Melanie.
10·98*

THE PERMANENT PRESS
SAG HARBOR, NEW YORK 11963

Copyright 1996 by Melanie Braverman

Library of Congress Cataloging-in-Publication Data

Braverman, Melanie, 1960-
　　East Justice/by Melanie Braverman
　　　　p.　　cm.
　　ISBN 1-877946-72-9
　　I. Title.
　　PS3552.R3556E27　　1996
　　813' .54--dc20　　　　　　　　　　　　　95-16897
　　　　　　　　　　　　　　　　　　　　　　CIP

All rights reserved, including the right to reproduce this book, or parts thereof, in any form, except for the inclusion of brief quotes in a review.

Manufactured in the United States of America

First edition, 1200 copies

THE PERMANENT PRESS
Noyac Road
Sag Harbor, NY 11963

For Sal

for my real family: Bob, Robyn, Tom, and Mac Braverman
and especially for my mother, June Braverman

Many, many thanks to Deborah Artman, reader and editor
extraordinaire; Louise Rafkin, Margaret Erhart, Ellen
Anthony, and Sarah Randolph, my weekly writing friends,
Candice Reffe; Bonnie Friedman; Steve Kaye; and my agent
Edite Kroll.

Portions of this book have appeared in *The American Voice*.

Once I was a bird, flying into the hands of trees. These days I am at watch in the narrative sky, petroglyph in a garden of cloud. In a dream, five small birds lay flightless on the floor, smothered and the color of my personal blood. What starts me awake at night begins as a ringing in the ears, sounds of mice foraging in the kitchen. Do I kill them? I try: there seems to be no end to their feeding.

I have the tongue of a bird in my mouth, narrow and short, cauterized by a lamp my father repaired. I was only three, he'd removed the broken socket and plugged the black cord into the wall to test the light. I put one end in my mouth, the taste still so vivid when I press my tongue's blunt edge against my teeth I feel an urgency there, something dry and white on the palate like salt, which I crave. To weep is to remember.

What is to remember? I came back to Iowa, took a place, settled in. But nothing lay between the field and the house, nothing of my life was visible in the black and fallow dirt. I put a chair beneath the window and from there in winter I set to work, fabrics and plumage and all manner of remnants to stitch into quilts. Panel by panel I've been courting this, as if the past were a shy animal come to feed silently in the yard. I make myself invisible to it behind the white blind of my house. As with the birds and deer I set out food for the past, offering my own self up because I believe the past desires me as much as I desire it.

We lived in the town of East Justice, National Guardsmen parading through the street summer Thursdays. Rifles twirling and flashing in the sun like teeth, local dogs darting in and out of the procession. The grass was green as green and the snow cones in the hands of the children were blue, unnatural as the sky those days: electric, some deeper shade of blue on our tongues.

There is an Eastern European folk song I know called "I Will Not Be Sad in This World." It is a wail and howl of voices unaccompanied by instrumentation. When a cyclone hits it sings this song and one's house is swept up in it or not by chance, the luck of the next door neighbors huddled in the cellar by torchlight. In this case we were always that saved family, we emerged those mornings blinking like moles in the unsuspicious light, open-mouthed at the damage around us: the Millers' roof in our front yard, or the Thompsons' biggest elm, roots and all, as if it wished to be replanted there. My mother made casseroles for the bewildered families, guilty and relieved over our good luck. "Like my parents," she would say, closing our unsplintered front door when she got home, "survivors," she'd pronounce us, we were very lucky. Days later when the street was clear of debris, the neighbor ladies came to return my mother's dishes. I stared at each of them from behind the front room drapes trying to discern their difference, but they looked like my mother in their printed shifts and sneakers, they did not look unlucky to me.

I asked my grandmother. "There is a piece of wood on your doorpost," she said. "God sees it and bad luck passes you by."

"Can't the Millers get one?" I asked her.

"No," my grandmother said. She drank tea from a glass and the spoon rang against its side like an instrument. Sun shone through the tea casting an amber shadow on the almond table.

My name is Grace.

When I was a girl I inhabited the top floor of our house as if I were an angel, too spare, too light for the ground floor. Four-leaf clovers of light came through the quatrefoil window, it was good luck from the sun and moon that spilled like milk onto the floor. I imagined my hair to be gold like the light. I drank cold water and ate salted peanuts from a glass bowl, and in the winter my mother brought me tangerines whose skins came away all of a piece in my hand. There were boxes of books written in a language I couldn't understand, but I could sleep all day if I liked. This was heaven, say, and I was an angel with wings and yellow hair, like stars.

When I finish a square I hang it on my wall, and so my house moves from austere to flagrant as the weeks go by. As I am at the beginning of a quilt, the wall is only part-way full, the few blue squares against the white paint like an inverse, cornered sky. When I am cleaning, when I am resting, when I eat my meal in the afternoon, I face the wall and study what it is I've made. Lately my eye has begun to dwell not on the fabric but on the white beyond, the odd-shaped space my handiwork does not fill, and there it remains until I remember to put the spoon in my mouth, and the food that ends up there is cold.

The river was rough and the poison in the river was invisible. To float, to float along the banks in an innertube in a suit with a yellow skirt like petals. My brother said, "I dare you to put your head under," but I ignored him. "Dare you," my brother said. He dove under the water and came up inside my tube, put his freckled hand on the crown of my head and pushed. I remember his blue feet, bubbles clung to his legs like flies. My head grew big and I thrashed my arms around involuntarily. It felt like we would go on like that forever, like marionettes my brother and I. I never thought I would die there. I believed we would live forever in the water.

I was untouched and I was tender.

I was not simple, I was beautiful pacing the stubbly fields in the afternoon. Farmers allowed their pigs into the corn post-harvest and I grew to associate the scent of droppings with the rattle and snap of drying stalks beneath my feet. I kept a bird on my shoulder those warm days who filled my head with ideas and pecked at the glass studs in my ears as I walked. When the sky caught fire it was time to rouse my grandmother for supper. Death to her was someone come to wake you, someone I did not want to be mistaken for, so I'd lean over her left shoulder and muster my nicest, my lightest, voice. "It's me," I'd whisper to my grandmother, "it's not what you think, it's time for supper." She'd swing her old legs over the side of the bed, fixing the white chenille spread to look as if she had not slept there.

"Put that bird away," she'd say.

I wanted to be light, I wanted to be kind, I wanted to be on a winning team. I wanted benevolence and good fortune, I plucked and pulled at my fleshy middle and did not recognize myself in pictures. Mother cooked and we ate and afterward I cleared away the dishes.

"How was school?" my dad would ask and I would tell him, "Fine."

"Right," my brother said, scorn in his mouth like the gristle I chewed and chewed washing up. I picked fat off the plates and dipped it in salt and ate it standing at the sink, letting the warmish water soothe my hands. I wanted nothing abstract: I wanted a baby, I wanted long hair, I wanted to play the piano without trying, without practice. I wanted my brother to be nice to me. I liked to pull the plug from the sink after washing, to watch the water whirl itself down the drain, neatly, away.

Once a twister came to pluck me like a rabbit from sleep, screech of a song in its throaty middle. I woke that night screaming, they tell me, running the length of the upstairs hall, frantic. My father caught me, Mother ran a cold bath and plunged me in. The tub was white the tile was yellow my skin shrank like an animal's the light was blue as if through ice I thought, returning. My mother bathed my cheek like a pragmatist, my father had already disappeared. They never asked me anything, just lowered a fresh night-gown over my head and kept the hall light burning beneath my door. Only my grandmother, shaking her head at the table the next morning as if she knew what swallows one whole in the night. She was letting her dyed-red hair go gray, and without rouge looked like a woman turning by the hour to stone.

"What?" I asked her.

"Eat your oatmeal," she told me, "a dream, it was nothing."

She was spooning food into her mouth. She was humming.

"When the cossacks came we were packed and ready to go, we did not wait for them to push us out into the streets like dogs," my grandmother said.

I brought her a smoked fish on a blue plate. I sat down.

"I was the smallest," she said, "my place was on top of the wagon, perched up there level with the eyes of the handsome soldiers. The breath of their white horses came out as white clouds, and I remember the sun feeling warm on my back. I had to pass water but I was too afraid to ask my mother to stop and let me down, and besides, even then I was too proud to squat in front of the soldiers. 'Move on,' the cossacks said and so we moved."

My grandmother ate the skin of the fish, its soft white fat, its flesh.

"The house of my mother's brothers smelled of wood smoke and bachelorhood. We had come a long way to their village, the uncles offered tea but had, they sighed, no sugar to give their only sister. 'Tea without sugar is for peasants,' my mother said, we were a good family, cultured, even our meals of boiled potatoes looked fine with their sprigs of wild onion. My sister fetched the sugar from the wagon, the curve of my bottom impressed on the sack where I'd sat that whole long trip. My uncle slit its off-colored cloth and scooped sugar into a chipped china bowl, but to our surprise the sugar was yellow instead of white, lumpy instead of smooth as it passed through his hand. 'Spoiled?' my uncle asked, stroking his smelly old beard. 'Nonsense,' my mother scolded, 'sugar is sugar,' spooning some into her cup, and then some more. I squirmed in my seat and she swatted at my head like a fly till I stopped."

"What did you do?" I asked my grandmother. She'd picked up the skeleton of the fish between her hands like an ear of corn and was sucking the last of the flesh from the bones.

"I asked for tea," she said.

"But Yaya," I said, "the sugar!"

She took an apple from a wooden bowl and began to peel it slowly with the sharp knife she kept in the pocket of her housedress, red skin coiling onto the blue plate like a spring.

"What is good enough for the mother is adequate for the

child," she said, slicing a wedge from the core of the apple and offering it to me without even looking my way.

I was bound to my mother like a fish forever on the line, running with, then against, the current. Black hair, brown eyes, an animal nose sharp and honking with allergies every season, my hand fit around her small wrist and she was glad to wear me through the aisles of the IGA like a jewel. She had a charm bracelet she wore when she got dressed up, one gold head for each of her children, a mustard seed under glass, a dollar bill folded tight inside a tiny silver cube. The handles of her blond wood dresser were bone-shaped and brassy in the light, and they caught the glint of her bracelet as she posed in front of the tall mirror eyeing herself the way a stranger might, a look that was not meant for me. I ran my hands through pairs of panty hose from her bottom drawer searching for a pair without runs, helping. The TV was on, a TV I had won as a baby when my father entered my name in a local drawing, but everything I had belonged first of all to my mother. She smelled of lipstick and powder though the smell of frying onions clung to her cool hands, reclaiming her as she patted my face on her way out of the room. I stayed on her bed long after she and my father left the house, feeling the cord between us tighten the further away she pulled.

"Someday you'll be glad to be away from me," she'd say when at last she came home to find me asleep on her side of the bed with my arm inside the leg of a stocking.

My father left for work early each day, not a farmer but a lover of farms, a merchant selling implements to the yellow haired fathers of my peers. His desk sat atop a low pedestal in the showroom and Saturday mornings I spent rummaging its noisy metal drawers for sticks of gum and sour candies that made me suck my cheeks in like my father's imitation of a fish. At noontime he locked the door with a key from among a collection of keys, and I fondled the heavy ring like an amulet where it hung from the ignition while he drove. Some days home, others out into the country where he took us to visit a Mennonite family who raised parakeets and tropical fish, peacocks and puppies that performed for us in the outside pens, trying to catch our eye as we climbed, my family and I, from the car. The lights were dim in the aisles of fish, and we wandered among the tanks like foreigners prolonging the moment when our father called upon us to choose. My brother liked a fish that trailed violet plumes as it swam and would fight with its mate to the death if it could, a proud fish, expensive and alone. My father liked the angels and my sister chose the pink gouramis, she was older than me, she liked the way they kissed like people open-eyed, they made us blush. I loved the fish that schooled the best, all of them looking like one fish as they darted back and forth across the tank. Each visit my eyes came to settle on the neon tetras, electric blue and magenta, the colors I saw behind my eyes when I closed them. Loosed next day from their halfway house of plastic bags, my new fish swam into the midst of the old school and disappeared, indistinguishable, the effect of the mass swelling as subtle as the deepening hours of sleep.

We drove Old County through So Long to town, passing the Johnson's farm on our right with the billboard of Jesus that says TIME ENDS. Further down another billboard Jesus marked the border of the Johnson place. ETERNITY WHERE was all it said and I'd spend the rest of the ride into town trying to figure that out, rolling the strange words around in my mouth like exotic fruits: *Jesus Lutheran Christian Christ.*

Once I was invited to Larry Johnson's house in the spring. He raised goats for the 4H Fair and wore checked shirts and work boots to school. We sat at their kitchen table eating bacon and egg sandwiches and watched the roller derby on TV until it was time to help his older brother with the pigs. We went to the barn and filled four buckets with corn, then waited in the feeding pen for the sows to be let in for their dinner.

"You should take Jesus into your heart," Larry said.

"How?" I said. I could hear the nursing sows shriek and pace, more ravenous the closer they got to the pen.

"Let me feel your head first," he whispered.

"Why?" I asked.

"Just do it," he said. He put his buckets down and approached me as if I were an animal he did not want to scare. He fixed his eyes on mine and came closer. He put his hands on my head. He moved his fingers slowly around my scalp, searching for something encoded there, some message waiting to be discerned. I closed my eyes. My heart beat fast and I thought I felt a little door opening between my ribs the way in fairy tales a door emerges from some seamless face of stone, and I thought I felt the Jesus from the billboard enter the door with his bare feet and his sad face, and I thought he would be warm inside my heart, happy to be out of the weather. "They're supposed to be like my goat's," Larry was saying, groping my head, "but I don't feel anything there." Then the gate to the pen slid

14

back and a drift of hogs rushed to make an island of us both, and without a thought I flew headfirst like a pigeon to roost on the shed roof of the feeder. Larry Johnson was a little boy down there among the feeding pigs.

"You're not a Jew!" he yelled up at me.

I sat in our kitchen watching my grandmother dress chickens for Friday night. She had a cleaver only she could use, not even my mother was allowed to pick it up. It had come over on the boat, my grandmother said, as if that knife were a person, as if it had a life of its own. Its haft fit perfectly in her blunt hand, like a glove she said each time she picked it up. She raised her billowy arm and off came the chickens' heads, their necks, their yellow, scaly feet. She reached up inside the chickens and out the bundles of organs came.

"Gross!" I said as she tossed the oddest parts into a pot.

"Everything is useful," she told me, wiping her hands on an old kitchen towel, strafing the bleached-out cotton with blood.

"Even the eyes?" I asked her, even the beak?

"Pah," my grandmother scolded me, "if you were hungry would you turn up your nose at soup?" cleaver nodding in her hand as she talked.

My friend was an Japanese girl from California, she had a heart-shaped mouth and narrow eyes and black hair that would grow to the floor if it wasn't cut back every so often like grass. Her mother stirred soup with sticks instead of a spoon and when she got mad her voice turned shrill and scolding as a cricket's. I never saw the adults in that house eat, they fed us fried chicken and string beans before sitting down to their private, fishy-smelling meals. I felt so big at their table those nights they invited me to stay for supper, larger even than the tiny dad who sometimes came to sit in the kitchen silently while we ate. I wore a sundress printed with sunflowers that spring and we'd sit in the sandbox after supper, pouring sand through the funnels of our hands and not talking. All over the neighborhood screen doors slammed with kids coming out while they still could. A boy from across the street came and sat in the sandbox with us, his name was full of silent letters and he was older than us, his father owned the pizza place and his mother carried her Chihuahua through the neighborhood like a baby.

"What are you doing?" the boy asked, and we told him, "Nothing." He dug his fists into the sand, came up with a few earthworms and threw them down the front of my dress. I screamed and my face grew hot, the boy laughed, the boy went away, the crickets were everywhere shrieking. My friend's mother called to her and then she went away, too. I sat by myself on the swings for a while, kicking myself higher and higher into the shifting sky, the new grass damp against the soles of my feet. At home I took a washcloth to my skin and rubbed the touched places with soap before I went to bed. I tried to picture the earthworms burrowing in for the night, and I knew what we'd been taught in school about them was right: that they were good, that they made our life on earth possible. But I could not remove the feel of the worms there. They were cold fingers going down.

I liked East Justice but I loved So Long the best. So Long is a green hill in a green valley, lilacs sprouting from its sides like wings.

The road to So Long was distracted with hills, some that led into town and some that led out. Its main road curved down into a sharp valley, green and cool in the summer trees. Across a wooden bridge that spanned a narrow break in the river, then up another big rise the town of So Long appeared, straddling a steeply rounded hill, the nearest thing to a mountain we had. It was like driving into another country, I thought, what I imagined Europe to feel like, with all its elegant shade. The townspeople of So Long must have thought so, too, because they built their houses with peaked roofs that lent an alpine air to the place; they referred to their town as a village and some let sheep or goats graze in their yards to nibble among the tulips and the jonquils in spring.

After big snowfalls the villagers closed off their smaller roads, and kids came from all around to sled the So Long hills; early in the morning, station wagons with toboggans and sleds strapped on top crept toward town on their snow tires and chains, braving the icy roads. Some dads sledded outside with their kids, but most stayed inside the So Long Cafe, talking with each other, drinking coffee well into the afternoon, eating the soup of the day when they got hungry, folding and refolding the Sunday News. We drank hot chocolate when we came inside, cheeks burning from the weather and from running up the hills and flying in the face of the fast wind down again, my brother in front and me in the middle, my sister clinging to my bundled waist. By the time we went home the snowplows had come and made a dry gray surface of the road again, outlines of the salt they used dissolved in the shapes of clouds on the pavement.

Once my parents took us to the movies to see *The Sound of Music*. Though my father dozed and my brother complained, I sat so still my mother had to nudge me every so often to see if I was awake. It was my first unanimated movie, and all the way home my parents laughed at what I must have been thinking, silent as I was in the singing dark of the theater. "Never seen people so big," and, "charmed by the little puppets and goats," they laughed, and they weren't altogether wrong, alive with their notions of what the youngest thought. I just let my head lean against the cold window in the back seat and waited for us to come to the So Long road. Even though their hill was a poor relative of the mountains that filled the movie screen from beginning to end, and their houses were not mansions, or A-framed and clinging to the sides of the hill, I admired the people of So Long for having seen something beautiful once and tried to make that thing for themselves, instead of never having tried for it at all. It made me want to want things too, and as we drove home I closed my eyes and imagined I was a nun who sang, a brave woman who loved someone else's children well, and let them dance in the meadows when they pleased.

When I opened my eyes again the snow had turned lavender from the setting sun, and it wasn't long for the world now, it was early spring and the snow shone wet as glass along the road. The land flattened out around us and we pulled onto our street, and were home.

West Justice had a reservoir and a dairy barn with tin spires that dazzled in the sun like mirrors. In the reservoir jagged halves of trees stood up in the water black against the blue or white sky. All of the people there looked like cousins, their ancestors from a coastal village in Europe where every year giant turtles were pulled from the green sea and eaten. Inland the ritual came to take the form of a pig roast, and for one whole day late in summer the air around West Justice filled with the sweet smell of alder smoke, and salt reminiscent of the sea.

Pink houses lined the streets, front room curtains secured away from the clean glass as if a desire for privacy meant trouble. Huge elm trees stood in the yards protecting the houses from hailstones and an overzealous sun. One day red X's appeared on the trunks of the West Justice elms, and soon all the trees were dead from Dutch Elm Disease. Men came with chain saws to cut the dead trees down and then all the trees in West Justice were gone, pink house paint replaced by white aluminum siding the residents hosed down like cars in the summer.

We rode the old train there some Sundays to swim, my mother's straw baskets filled with towels and chicken sandwiches for lunch. I sat with my back against the dusty velvet seats of the train, hands splayed along the dark wooden armrests like the spokes of wheels. Velvet bristled the bare backs of my thighs like a cat's tongue and when I closed my eyes I dreamt I was a turtle flailing my legs in the hot sun. "Look out for the trees," my mother called each time we dove into the water.

Every night awakened by this dreaming: afloat in a sea I have never seen. Afloat, or grounded on a beach while great animals rise and sink like swells of prairie. Am I naked? Do I desire this? Do I dwell in the water? I am pushing a needle through fabric to earn my keep. The quilt I am making is solid blue (sea blue? azure? aquamarine?) whose scalloped stitching when turned upside down resembles what I remember of the waves.

Once I went outside and our whole street looked different to me, even the sky seemed blurry and soft-focused like some romantic movie of a sky. I ran the stairs to my room certain I'd forgotten to put on my glasses, skimming the laminated top of my dresser, the pillow, the pale sheets.

"What are you doing?" my mother asked from the doorway.

"I forgot my glasses," I said. I turned to face her.

"They're on your face," she said, "now go to school."

I stopped in the bathroom on my way down the stairs. I locked the door. There they were, tortoise-framed and square beneath my squared-off bangs. I took my glasses off. I pushed aside the soap dish and the toothpaste and sat cross-legged between the double sinks, staring straight into my blue eyes. *Who are you?* a voice inside me kept saying.

To be an only child, a foster child, an orphan. To be discovered by some mother and father grateful for a girl like me, mindful and mild as chamomile. I pretended to be found on a warm afternoon in autumn, fallen poplar leaves whispering my story as I walked. Sometime near my birthday so we'd have a celebration with white cake and lots of thoughtful gifts on the table. I'd be lovely but contented to wait. I'd have the straightest blonde hair in town, one look and everyone would figure out the dark-haired adults I lived with were not my own, their hook-nosed boy only posed as my brother, that spiteful, black-haired girl no sister of mine. I belonged with people who read books to one another by lamp light in the evening, said "thank-you" for no apparent reason and "lovely" and "I'm sorry." I sat in my attic reading *The Boxcar Children* and *Sensible Kate* over and over to myself. Set cookies outside in the evening to tempt those slender spirits home.

On Friday nights my grandmother wore a wig that lived a life of its own atop her thinning hair, happy to be off of the styrofoam head and allowed to dance in the breeze as we drove all together into town. Hair and lipstick slightly askew, she looked a little blurry those nights, and I'd let my eyes go in and out of focus on her when I got fidgety in the back seat of the Olds. Every Friday we went to town, and every Friday my grandmother rose during services to mourn the memory of my grandfather. Though I was just a little girl when he died, I could remember the cool pickle crocks he scrubbed and filled with brine in late August, the glads he grew and cut like swords for the table, the way he pinched my cheeks between his fingers like a vice. Now my grandfather was one of the commemorative lights that shone on the Eastern wall of the temple like a movie marquee, illuminating the brass name plates of all the other dead Jews from our towns. When at the end of the service everyone rose to face east toward Jerusalem, I believed those personal lights served to show the way to that mythical place, that foreign home where my grandfather still made pickles and pinched the cheeks of angels. And though she cursed him almost daily under her breath, my grandmother sang the mourner's *kaddish* with her eyes straight ahead on the altar like arrows fixed on God, and swiped at my grandfather's name plate with a kleenex as she went down the stairs to eat cake.

Ours was a small temple built along a creek, and in spring the boys rolled their good pants up around their knees and caught crawdads while the girls picked violets for their mothers. The ladies were back-combed and straight-backed, the men all restless in their dark suits, eager to be out in the lobby having a smoke. The Silversteins, the Davidsons, the Goldbergs; the Weisenbergs, the Milkens, and Mrs. Oppenheimer who sang louder than anyone, deep-chested and kindly next to her quiet husband, George. We had poppy seed cake and red punch in the basement of the temple once a week, except those springs when the rains made the creek jump its banks; then the basement was flooded and musty, the rabbi spoke about Noah in his sermons, and we took our refreshment under the glare of spotlights on the higher ground of the front lawn.

Once in midsummer I sat in the sanctuary by myself after the service. The seats in our temple shifted like the ones in fancy theaters, and I tipped myself back to watch the light from the setting sun bounce through the glass onto the golden cover of the ark. I was thinking about the eternal light which flickered daringly each time the congregation rose and sat. I was thinking about what language God spoke in his everyday life, Hebrew or English. I had drawn a picture of God for myself, one half man in a navy blue suit and one half woman in paisley, my favorite print. It was just for reference, in order to have a clear image in mind when we had our conversations, which was like praying to me. Maybe one half speaks Hebrew and the other English, I was thinking. I closed my eyes, then opened them. "Dear God," I said. "It's me, it's Grace here." The man side of God straightened his tie, the woman side smiled off into the distance. Then a little bat rustled its wings and flew down from the temple rafters, circled and returned to its roost. I'd been watching that bat all evening; that bat was the reason I'd stayed behind after all the others had gone downstairs for cake. *"Boruch atah adonai,"* I tried again. The man God turned his face in my direction.

I braided my sister's hair on the riverbank, pulling the thick sections back from her forehead shiny and curved as the moon. Usually I annoyed my sister, but sometimes, when the sun went down and we were alone, she turned friendly again, as if the violet in the sky changed me into someone she didn't mind. She talked to me then, the way our mother talked to her hairdresser on Friday afternoons, like I was her most intimate friend, not the one you hung around with but the one you most often told the truth to.

"Janet Sawyer's a bitch," my sister said. She didn't come down to the river so much anymore, and when she did I wanted to make it last; I plaited her dark hair to the end, messed it up, started over.

"But she's your best friend," I said.

"Duh," my sister said, splashing her toes in the water.

I undid the braid. "I'm sorry," I said. "About Janet and

all." I dug down through her hair and flexed my fingers against her scalp like a cat's, which she liked.

"Me, too," she said, leaning her whole body deeper into the half-circle of my own. "But thanks."

We took our time going home that night, throwing pebbles into the river, running our fingers along the tops of the fine, tall grass. After supper we lay in bed in our shared pink room listening to the June bugs hurl themselves against the screen, determined and insistent, wanting so much to get in.

My brother was a hobo with a penciled stubble on his chin, my sister wore a packaged monster suit we'd picked up for her at Kresge's over the weekend. My mother's lipstick and filmy scarves made me into a princess for Halloween, and I played those scarves across the floor all afternoon like leashed pets, cooing to them, teasing them, shaking them seductively along at my heels. My father came home early with two boxes of candy tucked under his arms. We scooted our supper around on our plates, saving ourselves for the evening's spoils, while my grandmother ate all of her baked chicken and beans, afterward claiming her private box of candy from my father and taking her seat at the front room glass, putting chocolates in her mouth with her hooked hands, waiting. It was the only American holiday she liked and she took her position by the door seriously, surveying each child's costume with a critical eye, demanding entertainment until, satisfied at last, she plunked two treats into each outstretched sack instead of one. For this reason the neighborhood kids clamored to our door, but late in their rounds, hoping to catch my grandmother tired of all the ceremony but generous, still, with her treats.

I was to go trick-or-treating with my friend that night, a

black girl named Rita who lived next door. Rita was a tall girl whose strict mom made her wear long skirts and anklets to school and oil her hair every day, encouraging the cluster of little pimples that ranged her shiny brow. "Ungrateful devil," Rita's mother would say whenever Rita struggled under the tug of the metal comb. Rita's mother was a firm believer in manners and when I ate lunch there we sat with our feet squarely on the floor, napkins in our laps, eating the soup first and sandwich second, and potato chips from a crystal bowl that sat in the middle of their fancy table. Rita was shy and deferential near adults but when we were alone she turned into a regular girl, flinging her Barbies across the room to simulate flight, wanting to be a crossing guard at school. "My mother is a witch," Rita would say, but I didn't think she was all that bad; she cleaned up Rita's room for her and made her Halloween costumes from scratch, long sheaves of taffeta and a little hat with veils, studded all over with shiny beads of silver and pearl.

It was cold that day and by three o'clock snow was falling in thick medallions on our street. By four o'clock a good inch covered the pavement, and by five the limbs of the trees hung low, surprised to be bearing such weight so early in the season. Then the snow stopped and stars broke through the clouds, and the moon joined league with the jack-o-lanterns on our porch to cast a yellow light on the snow. After our mothers conferred on the phone, Rita and I were allowed to set off, having agreed to wear snow pants and mittens beneath our sheer gowns. I pinned my scarves to the shoulders of my winter coat and insisted on wearing lipstick despite my muffler, the smell of it coming back to me with each steamy breath, helping me feel more princess-like, more light on my feet despite the weight of my rubber boots. Rita's mother made her wear her jacket on the out-side, but once out of sight Rita flung it into her paper sack. The street lights on her brown face shimmered like wind on a still pond, and with her silver breath and flowing sleeves she was the most beautiful girl I'd ever seen. "Your mother's gonna kill you," I said to Rita, and she said, "I don't care."

"What are *you* supposed to be?" the ladies would ask me as they answered their doors; it must have been obvious to them what Rita was, though, they never asked her a thing.

"Trick or treat," we'd mumble through our layers, and when someone asked us for a trick we'd fall backward in the snow, offering up two angels in trade that seemed to fly up from the ground as we lifted our bodies carefully and backed away, not wanting to mess their fragile shapes.

By eight o'clock our sacks were full and we turned the nearest corner to home, dragging our load behind us on a sled we'd had the good idea to bring along. We scooped snowballs into our mittens, tossing them to the side as we went like crumbs to mark the way, and it was as if we were alone on the street that night, though of course other children were out there too, lost in their own enchantment. Rita's laugh diminished as we reached her front door, where her mother ushered her in and said good night and sent me on. I stopped on our porch for one last look before going inside; I watched the outlines of costumed children padding quietly but quickly with their heavy sacks, ghosts coalescing between the constellations and the snow.

The trees sway drunk with movement, maudlin and jealous of the birds' wings. A brace of wild turkey comes, flightless and silly, headfirst through the brush. What is there really to wish for? I pass among them all, neither rooted nor mobile in the autumn woods, gathering chestnuts, gathering the brightly molted feathers.

I lay on an old coffee table my father was supposed to refinish for my mother, the dusty surface smooth against the backs of my legs, which were bare.

"We are going to play a game," my brother said.

His face looked odd staring down at me, like a cliff diver ready to hurl himself over the edge into the water, and it made me feel dizzy to look up at him like that. I closed my eyes. He raised my dress. He moved my flowered underpants over to one side and touched my vagina with the rubber end of a pencil, it was scientific, he said, he did not like to dirty his hands. I lay still, I lay flat on my back. It was damp in the basement and though it was August I felt a chill, but wherever the pencil touched me was warm, as if that pencil were dividing me piece by piece, as if the different parts of my body were taking up sides against one another. "Is this good?" my brother whispered to me, moving the pencil back and forth, like I was being erased down there.

My aunts came, my cousins came, from down the block and far away as Minnesota. We went to the beauty shop, I got a new dress, my mother hired Celeste and Anita Bope from the temple to come in their crisp aprons and serve chopped liver to the guests. They'd worked for the temple since before I was born, receiving the ladies' baked goods on Friday afternoons before the service, slicing cakes, making punch. They had white hair and never married, the only twins I'd ever known, identical glasses hanging from jewelled chains around their necks. They snapped their gum and clucked their tongues when the old men pushed through the swinging doors to add a nip of schnapps to their coffee. "Devil's work," Anita would say, washing glasses in the double sink as Celeste arranged cookies on platters.

The sisters were Christian but they were fond of me, they let me pick the cashews from the big cans of nuts and listen to them gossip about people I didn't know, poking me in the ribs as they straightened their hair and took food out to the tables for the guests. I liked to stay with them in the temple kitchen during parties, perched on a stool at the red formica counter, sucking ice cubes with my little tongue. But tonight I was not allowed in the kitchen. Now I was twelve and that evening would stand before our congregation and take what was coming, bless us all in a language I did not understand and light candles with a shaking hand. The Bopes served dinner on my mother's good china and my sister drank wine on the sly with Sarah Stein. I sipped my mother's clear soup and nothing else, trying not to think about the future.

The rabbi had a big belly and a long red beard, his wife was short, they smelled of perspiration and an overabundance of hair. Their name was Abramson and they were new to our town, hungry all the time and foreign as fish. Besides my grandmother they were the only ones who called me by my Hebrew name; Grace, the rabbi said, was as *traif* as they come, calling me Gittl in class when he chose me to recite. He made a tape for me of the prayers whose melodies I was supposed to learn by heart. I sat in the attic watching the reels turn round and round, losing myself in his scratchy, nasal incantations. I learned to jump my voice like a frog, to make the quick loops down and hold other notes just so. I listened until the melodies felt like a map to me, inflecting as I practiced toward a meaning based on the way the sounds felt to make them, a keening and complaint like migrating birds, a little homelessness in the back of the throat. When I got around to reading the translation it was news to me, nothing like what I imagined or felt. In the end I abandoned the English altogether, preparing my mandatory speech around the easy subject of what I knew adults would like to hear, a gift from me in exchange for the savings bonds and fancy ball point pens. *Thank you for coming*, I imagined myself saying, *I hope one day to be just like you.*

I was the first girl in our *schul* to carry the Torah, and I fell asleep at night foreseeing my fateful fall from the *bimah*, sacred scrolls unfurling as the pointer jangled to the floor. Forty days and forty nights of fasting was the punishment, and I'd wake from that dream panting and hungry, the thick tongue of the rabbi clucking in my ears. When the time came, though, I was sure-footed as a horse, lifted from myself by the solemn way the adults touched their prayer books to the Torah and pressed the black spines to their lips, more gently than they would a dying woman, plump or bony fingers and *tallis* fringes stretching out as if it was me they wanted to touch. The silver breastplate clanked rhythmically against the scrolls as I walked, and when I rounded the last turn I caught my grandmother out the corner of one eye, shaking her head back and forth with her eyes wide open and smiling for a change, happy to look upon a young girl cradling the word of God in her arms like a baby.

I handed the Torah over to the rabbi and sat down. Then began the calling of the names, my father and uncles rising to the call, one by one approaching the altar, singing their parts in a quavering voice, children once more in the shadow of the Lord. And when my turn came to say my piece I was braver than even my father had been, I knew my part and sang it out as if I were alone in the attic with just the rabbi's voice to lead me on. This time, though, I could lead myself. My dress was white and my hair was just beginning to grow out, I wore nylon hose and patent shoes and songs flew out of my mouth to hang like stars in the temple sky. When I was finished the rabbi bent to kiss my cheek. I remember the scratch of his beard on my face and the heat of his breath coming near. I was shocked. I looked ahead. My grand-mother had tears in her eyes and my mother was crying too. My father wore a distant smile on his face, clapping my mother over and over on the back like she was sick.

Afterward we drank fizzy punch and ate *petits fours* with my initials iced in blue across the tops. Rita was there, and other friends from school, the boys subdued in their clip-on ties and slip-on shoes, pale and small-featured against the backdrop of Jews. We stood around with mono-grammed napkins in our hands. They acted as if I were a tenth-grader or a teacher, during the service I'd become a mystery to them all, they were hushed and still in my pres-ence and full of notions they'd go over later when I was no longer around. "That was really cool," one of the girls said to me, and I replied, "Thanks." They had no idea what I'd done but they'd pooled their money and bought me a gift anyway, and standing there among them I opened the little box. Inside was a silver I.D. bracelet, *Grace* etched across its face in script. *Good luck*, it said across the back. I put it on and held out my hand and Rita hitched the clasp with her slender nails. "Gittl," the rabbi called and I let my hands fall to my side, facing the doorway where my rela-tives were spilling forth like rain. The hand with the bracelet felt weighted by the cool metal, inclining me slightly toward my friends as I turned. "Who?" they asked as I faced in the direction of my name.

I'd been given a stuffed walrus big as a German shep-herd, blue and plush with white tusks and plastic eyes, sad and resigned as an orphan. I loved that thing and took him to bed with me at night, I was a grown-up now but I didn't care, I'd begun to feel things that set me apart whether I played with dolls or not. I'd heard my sister rummaging around in her bed at night, and I knew she was awake with herself and I knew enough to keep quiet. The covers made a rustling sound as if she wasn't alone in there, and after a while she'd moan and roll over and sleep. We lay awake at night, my walrus and I, listening and listening to my sister. Her noise sent a shiver rushing beneath my skin, and when I slept I dreamt the walrus read my thoughts and liked all the same things as me, the fineness of his blue fur a secret I could touch and touch forever.

One morning when I woke from this dream I felt an urging below my belly as if I had to pee, but when I went to the bathroom I wasn't relieved at all, and lay in bed twitching softly from the hips, a wooden puppet whose joints were hinged with string. I moved my hand down to where the urging seemed to be, and the feeling seemed to retreat and grow greedy with my hand there, coaxing my hand down below my waist. The further I went the more focused the feeling became, like the aperture of a camera that narrows and narrows to get its shot, until the feeling seemed to emanate from a spot the size of a pencil tip, and I touched myself there. Something exploded inside of me, I bucked from the hips and then, in a few seconds, my legs stopped twitching, I lay there limp and breathing hard and I knew I had located the source of my sister's restlessness.

"Come down," my mother called when it was time for breakfast, but for once I let hunger settle deep in me some. I stayed in bed for a long time, letting my hand come again and again to that little spot, but it never felt the same as it had the first time I touched myself there.

Now I cut flowers for the weekend market which the town ladies buy for their breakfronts and solid tables. Zinnias I cut, hollyhocks and asters, baby's breath and chrysanthemums and yellow everlastings. Tie my hair back, put a dress on, fill my pockets with change that will keep me weighted and connected to the ground, that muscle just beneath the asphalt lot where I'll yellow my skirt with pollen as I wrap up the bundles of flowers. Here comes Mrs. Hockmuth, I feel the height in her intention, she buys gladiolus and sunflowers for her showy sunroom. Liza Quinn, dressed as a man, shops for nasturtiums for her salads, spider bites hidden among the cool taste of the greens. "I am going on a long journey," Mr. Wilhite tells me, choosing a bunch of scarlet apologia for his wife. "Grace," he says formally, screening his eyes from the sun and moves on. It's the end of things, but no one's listening; ladies' skirts are switching back and forth between the aisles of peddlars as if this were the IGA, strawberries and sweet corn when the children say they want some for supper. I haven't had forget-me-nots since June but they are what Mr. Wilhite asks for first. It's a seasonal thing, I tell him, and this is the end, this is what ties us to ourselves, but no one listens. Below my dirty feet something physical takes a breath and remembers, something burnt and unworried by what is coming. Two white dahlias I have to take home. I bring them in, the six o'clock sky already turning.

I came home from the river to find my sister alone in the front grass scowling. She wore red shorts and a striped top, with her dark hair she looked like a red-winged blackbird clinging to corn in a field. "What's wrong?" I asked her.

"Dad's left," she said.

"To where?" I asked, picturing him on the road to Des Moines for a tractor show, wind messing the part in his thinning hair.

"Just gone," she said, "ask Mom if you don't believe me."

The day was blue and hot, fine hairs clung to my face and neck like leaves. I shook my head hard. I went inside. I went to my mother's door and looked around. She was sitting on the edge of her bed tearing a kleenex to bits in her hands. Bitterness had taken root in her face while I'd been out, haggard and pinched at the mouth and brow, a face I did not recognize and was afraid of. I began to cry. She stroked my face and wetted my hair with her tears. "Please don't," she said over and over in my ear.

I was in the basement of our house watching the day spill cross-hatched through the window wells, lily-of-the-valley and money plants silhouetted against the dusty glass. Canned goods filled the metal shelves rusting in the neglected air, a larder my mother had long refused to enter. Broken stools, broken lamps and broken toys, families of garter snakes spawning in the spring. Field mice and the conspiratorial sound of their running. Several seasons of flood down there. The hollow stairs. The orange walls. The smell of the memory of water in the napless rug. When I was mad I sat on the basement stairs, not wanting to go down there and not wanting to come back up. Outside, the shadowed plants described a cove in which I longed to dip my feet at night, wading calf-high to the high pines where fireflies suggested the many possible ways through the trees.

Last night the wind came to coax the last of the leaves from the trees, delivering me clean to the cusp of a different season. Now there are shadows like webs on the long north side of the house, the fingers of the trees fallen silent in an absence of wind. I spent the past week covering my garden with hay, and already I miss the neighborhood of plants, friendly and generous with leaves and pods. The dahlias and glads I dug out early, then potatoes before the ground could freeze, and now the Brussels sprouts are lonely things, adamant green against the yellow straw. I laid these beds to rest the way I have for five seasons now, spreading straw and fallen leaves over my black earth like a blanket. Today ten inches of snow in the far corner of the state. Coming again and again to sleep.

My brother ate grapefruits and lean meat and washed himself many times a day with green soap, leaving him pink in the face and smelling like medicine. He had an orange Toyota and spent longer and longer hours away from our house, running inside only to shower and drive away again, as if staying any longer than necessary meant harm to him, as if we meant to cause him harm. He spent his time at home with his door locked, whispering over the phone to girls with long, thin hair. If I lay just right on the attic floor, I couldn't make out the language but I heard the verdant promise in my brother's voice, trying to get those girls to want, to believe him. Soon he stopped using the front door altogether and took to climbing in his second-story window from the roof; years later, when a salesman bent on selling my mother new window sets came to our house, he displayed as proof of her need the screen my brother had pushed from its casing each night, bent and bowed like a muscle stretched beyond its original intent.

Once I was sitting on the milkbox watching a summer storm blow up when my brother came home and drove his car into the garage door, which was down. He stood there in the driveway, stunned and confused as a moth who still can't believe in the density of glass. "God," he said, rubbing his angry eyes. He looked at me. "I didn't see it," he said. "Shit," he yelled, and got back in his car and drove away.

I could hear my mother scrambling eggs and drinking coffee at the counter, scuffing back and forth in her slippers like a rasp.

"Mom," I called. "My stomach hurts, I can't go to school."

"You're not sick," she yelled back, disregarding as she did almost all of our complaints, empirical in her knowledge of the bodies of her children.

I closed my eyes and watched the blood-red veins move in my lids. "No really," I said, "I feel really bad."

"Get up," my mother said, "you'll feel better. Now move."

I took myself into the bathroom. I sat down and hung my hands between my legs. There were stains in my underpants where nothing was supposed to be, brown and warm like the spots of cows.

"Mom," I called, "there's something wrong."

She came into the bathroom. She laughed. "Nothing's wrong," she said, "you've done this before." She pulled a box from beneath the sink. My knees felt weak and I had a hard time breathing. I thought you only had to have a period once.

I took the box from her, turning it over and over like an artifact as I sat. The pads smelled of bleach and austerity, and I sat there for a long time going over how this whole thing worked. I had seen the explanatory film strips that fall; here was the recipe for babies, the film strip said, but how could I believe it? A woman's organs looked like the head of a cow to me, the sperm were greedy tadpoles, the egg too round to be an egg. When the lights came on I kept my eyes moving, not wanting to look at the teacher. "This is a tampon," Miss Letizio was saying. The cut-out groundhogs and spelling charts that lined the walls looked silly all of a sudden; what was it we were doing there, I thought, what was it we were supposed to be learning? I could hear the boys snickering in the room next door, high and nervous as liars. I must have missed some pertinent information that day, because when my first blood came, I believed that when it ran its course I would actually belong to myself again, familiar and undisturbed as a lake after skipping a stone.

It had snowed in the night, and my skin looked blue and sick in the milky light. I got a clean pair of underwear out and fixed a pad in place. I crawled back in bed and lay clenching and unclenching my toes, rubbing my feet together, nervous over a speech I had to give that day. It was for a contest the Rotary Club sponsored every year and every sixth-grader was assigned to compete. Each speech had to begin with the phrase *Give me your hand*, and I'd never once practiced mine out loud. I thought my outward voice would match the one in my head when the time came, my gestures falling into place naturally, like snowflakes or leaves. Now I wasn't so sure. I pulled the sheet up over my head and closed my eyes.

"Give me your hand," I whispered, rigid and wooden as a spoon.

Birds ride the dry grass pecking seeds from the heads of flowers. I imagine myself back in the time of the prairie, rolling and rolling into itself, unchecked by fences and barns.

There were onions to chop, there were lists to make, there were Mennonite girls who came to our house every Friday to clean. The Steins had Ruth and we had Inez, they drove a black car twenty miles each way, Ruth dropping Inez off at eight-thirty, fetching her at five to go home. Inez brought us Indian corn and cookies when she came, always glad to see us, to dwell in our loud house, a happy miner digging us out of the past week's slag. My mother told us to straighten our rooms before she came, but Inez didn't seem to mind picking up our clothes; I watched her finger the bright fabrics and girls' slacks as if they were treasures to her. Her dresses were pale, her eyes were dark, her dark hair coiled like a snake behind her shy head, tucked under a net cap that signified modesty in the eyes of God. Her mother was dead and her father was old, and he thought Inez wicked, she said, for taking her stockings off in summer to wade in the creek by her house, for being nineteen and unmarried and at ease. But Inez was the hardest-working person I knew. She wore glasses and finished her housework by noon, cleaning out cupboards and closets after lunch. I lay on the bench in the kitchen while she worked, listening to her hum and talk.

Inez took me to a wedding once where I filed into the church with the other women and, taking my cue, knelt on the hard boards along with everyone else until she put her cool hand on my neck and let me stop. There was cold chicken and kraut on the lawn after, and I sat with Inez on a quilt watching the Mennonite kids play, boys on one side and girls on the other. I peered over my glasses at Inez across the blanket. At home she was strange but here she was a plain face among the vast plain of her people. Her dress that day was lavender, she smelled human, she smelled of sweat and grass. The dress I wore seemed the obvious choice when I'd stood at my closet deciding: floor length, pale green, with yellow flowers hooked along its scoop neck. I had fixed my hair, I'd scrubbed my teeth, I wanted to be noticed but unseen that day, like everyone else, I thought, to stand out only a little. But when I stepped from Inez's black car at the church, I stood out like a stain there, showier even than the bride herself.

The curious passed by us steadily, peeking down to take me in before moving on to fill their paper plates. "I wish I looked like you," I said.

Inez just laughed. "But we all look alike," she said.

Soon Inez's father sent her off to teach orphans in Ohio and a new woman came to clean house for us, an immigrant with no English who ate bread and sugar and dark coffee for lunch. Inez sent us cards at holidays saying how happy she was, teaching geography, taking turns cooking supper for the other unmarried teachers at the school. She even sent a letter to me personally once. I never got mail, and I sat beneath the neighbors' willow tree staring like an idiot at the envelope, marvelling at my good luck. *The world is amazingly large*, she wrote. *Best regards to you from your friend, Inez.*

Years later, a yellow Volkswagen pulled up in my mother's drive. I was in the attic playing solitaire with an old deck of cards I'd found; I sat up and looked out the window. The driver of the car was a woman with short hair and long nails, made up and shadowed in low jeans and a red blouse. I crept down the stairs quietly after my mother answered the door. I watched from the dining room as the woman sat at the kitchen table with my mother, talking and drinking coffee, crossing and uncrossing her legs. "You inspired me," I heard her say, waving her arm around the messy room, heavy bracelets jangling like bells in the smoky air. I listened hard. I rubbed my eyes.

"What happened?" I asked this new Inez when finally my mother left the room.

She let go a thin stream of smoke from her mouth. "My father died, Grace," is what she said.

It is time to hunt and all the fields are filled with dangerous men, sipping brandy, sipping schnapps, conspiring in whispers with their anxious dogs. Neighbors bag pheasant and their wives hang and strip the birds clean as sheets in the back yard, feathers flying across the ground while the cats clean up, crazy and basic from the blood. Like boats at night the hunters toss and pitch about in their sleep, dreaming of the Dead Sea, all its unanchored contents afloat on its surface. No birds, no birds, not a bird in sight.

"Gittl, bring me an ashtray, and get your hair out of your face," my grandmother said. I did as I was told, crossing her room to the dresser, pushing my bangs off my face as I walked.

"You aren't supposed to be doing this you know," I said.

The middle fingers of her right hand were stained red from the smoking, and when she drew a Lucky from the pocket of her dress it stood out white there like a cloud in a painted sky. She tapped one end of the cigarette on the ashtray, which was a blue squirrel holding nuts on the edge of a pool, also blue.

"The only reason to quit is it costs too much," she told me, lighting up.

I held my breath as she held the smoke, itchy to see it come out, a dry stream. "Well, why don't you then?" I asked her, watching the powdery ash lengthen and sag.

"I don't pay," my grandmother said.

I sat on the foot of her bed, watching her old chest rise and fall. "Then let me try one," I said.

"No."

"Why?" I asked, plucking at the bedspread, letting my hair fall back down into my eyes.

"You are too young for smoking," she said.

"Younger than you when you first smoked?"

She took another drag, let her eyes graze the window, made a sigh.

"Just one," I said, "just a puff."

"Very well," my grandmother told me, "but not a peep to your mother."

"Promise," I said.

She pulled another Lucky out and handed it to me. The thin paper stuck to my lips, the taste of tobacco bitter and heady and high in my mouth. It was like eating steak, I thought. It was delicious. I struck a blue-tipped kitchen match against my shoe and held it to the cigarette, drawing the way I'd seen my grandmother draw so many times before. Smoke filled my mouth, my throat, my head, and soon I was coughing and feeling myself, deep in my body like a laughter that burns.

My grandmother laughed, taking the cigarette from my hand. "It's no good," she said, rubbing the cigarette out. She lay back on her pillow, shoved the ashtray into my hands, closed her eyes. I went into the bathroom and flushed the ashes away, saving the butts to take upstairs. I was dizzy and reeling from the toes on up, elated and foolish as an aerialist fallen to the net from her new trick.

I lay in bed, trying to imagine a place without winter. *Grace*, it calls, and I am not indifferent. It's just my mind is a heavy cloth in winter, encompassing a supine vocabulary only at night asleep in its boat of dreams. Still all over, no work except to lay as the fields lay, full of nothing but possibility. I open my eyes to my normal room: dresser, mirror, doorway, hall. White walls, window an ancient innovation toward hope, young girl in her mother's old dress. A monochromatic pallet is what lives out there, silencing and heavy with its burden of snow: gray sky, white land, the day just beginning to exist. *Ecstatic green*, I call to myself, held still beneath my heavy quilt, *green of poetry, green of plenty, remember me.*

What exists beyond these fields, flourishing in the further sky? Out here the eye can see far, but some days it is not enough. The door is open, the flat white glare of light I ask in like a guest to inhabit my rooms, fading the rugs, brandishing a sword to the dust. Tree limb and tree root, weighted with snow along the long drive. I know the heavy machinery of my neighbors sleeps in their barns, years of following the circular contours of fields accumulating great mileage from which they rest. As a child we drove to a lake in Minnesota, father at the wheel, mother navigating the small roads while we in the back fought and slept, indolent and moody as cats. We spent our two weeks swimming, pulling small perch from the lake, watching the fireworks my father and the other men ignited along the beach at night, too many at once so we'd run, shrieking, for the house.

"Do you like to go fast?" my father asked me one day on our trip when we were on our way into town for milk. He pressed his foot to the floor, one arm slung against the back of the seat, tapping a tune with the middle fingers of his hand. My face went white, a pale sheet watching the street lights rush by. "You're not scared!" my father said looking over at me, eyes glinting and wild as a boy's. He made the car go faster. I remember the warm vinyl of the seat, tacky and pinched where I clutched. This is my mother's seat, I thought. "This is fun!" my father said. I was only twelve but I reached for his arm. "Dad," I said in the calmest voice I had ever known. When he looked at me again his eyes had changed back, and he took his foot off the gas pedal, and slowed down.

On our way back home, my mother navigated us east to Illinois while my father listened to a ball game on the scratchy AM radio. "Damn it!" he yelled and banged the wheel with his palms when, blinking wide like a man woken up, he found out where we were. But I didn't mind. I'd been watching the road signs change for hours from one state symbol to the next, hoping the station wagon had somehow grown a mind of its own and was flinging us far afield whether we wanted to go or not.

Once after my father left I came home from school to find my mother in the front room by herself, doing nothing. She was fingering the heavy drapes, looking out the window at our narrow empty street.

"Wouldn't it be lovely to go away?" she said.

I lay my hand on my grandmother's face, holding it there like a blind girl new to Braille, taking my time to read the feathery skin. But only the wind came lowing across the plains, sweeping her voice up along with the topsoil and the wastepaper and the leaves. I rubbed my thumb across the surface of her cheek until I couldn't feel either anymore, and then there was nothing left to hold me to myself, feet dangling above the floor like a baby's when I propped myself next to my grandmother on the bed. The night before when I'd said good night, she'd told me a story about a man from her village, mad with grief at the loss of his wife, a girl with an indiscriminate smile who died giving birth to their one child. For days the man wandered from house to house, his pockets full of his wife's trinkets, banging on the doors of women who were touched by the man's grief and willing to overlook the filth of the hands thrust through their open doors, begging. The women asked the man in, sat him by their fires while he told them his story, and fed him what they had in the house, which was not much in those days, a slice of bread perhaps, a cup of broth.

One day as he was fumbling along, the man found a clay jug in the road. He pissed in the dirt, stirred with a stick, and with the mud he'd made began to plaster his wife's few things to the jug: her thimble, her hairpin, the spoon that had last fed her lovely mouth. Ever after, when the man sat by the fires of the village women, he held the jug to the flickering light, pointing from object to object, telling.

Years passed, and still the man wandered the village, begging bread, begging soup. One day he knocked on a door, only to find smiling at him the face of his long dead wife. So taken aback was he that he forgot all about the rumbling in his belly and stared for a long moment at the woman's face.

"And then what?" I asked my grandmother, kicking my heels anxiously against the side of her bed.

"What happens to everyone," she said. "He died."

"What?" I demanded.

"The truth," she said, patting the sheets with the palms of her hands.

"But who was she?" I said.

"Who knows?" my grandmother said, but I wanted to know. This is a story, I thought, she could be nice for a change, she could make things come out right.

"But the woman still had the jug," I said.

She wrapped her knuckly hand around mine, looking me square in the face as she talked. "Gittl," she said, "you're not a child anymore. The jug was nothing, piss and mud. The story died with the man," she said. "And the story," my grandmother told me, "was everything."

I went to bed and dreamed I was a salmon that night, silver and pink against the clear gray skin of a brook. But instead of having to struggle against the current I only ever had to swim downstream, allowing gravity to hurl me toward some easy end. I don't have to forgive you, I thought as I fell asleep.

Now I reached over and opened the window and invited every bird I saw to fly in the room and talk to me, to fill the shell of my grandmother with their little exhalations and crusts of bread. But her spirit had already shaken itself free and fled our house like a hobo bent for the thrill of the road. There was my mother outside the door, asking for me to let her in. "Open up," she was calling to me, "open up."

Already the house was filling with people and their food. And men had come to take my grandmother, to take my grandmother away.

I do not know where my mother has gone. This rocking has become my mother, these glassy eyes blinking from the motion like a doll's. My father has reappeared, pleading with my mother in quiet tones. But I am not fooled by his presence, he hasn't really come home. Those hands in his pockets are angry, the pulse at his temple is not his breathing but the sign of a clamping jaw. When did I learn to identify this, how did it happen? I am wearing a purple cardigan sweater, I pluck the little balls from my elbows, scooping out little breaths from my chest while my mother propels herself further and further away, as if pumping her legs on a swing. She doesn't say anything, she doesn't even smoke. A woman comes and pulls me from the room, puts a paper plate in my hand, says, "Eat." But soon I am back at my mother's door, watching her, trying to map which way she's gone so when she sends for me I'll pick up the trail, I'll go.

We used to call it *sit and shiver* before it ever happened to us. Now the house was full of women every day, come with bundt cakes from the temple to sit though the long afternoons in our house, fixing weak coffee and whispering among themselves, picking at the trays of cold cuts that occupied our kitchen table. Neighbors brought casseroles by, afraid to step through the front door as if the breath-heated air inside was itself of a different stripe, perhaps incompatible with their Gentile lungs.

We sat at a card table, my sister and I, and put a jigsaw puzzle together, one of a panda bear sitting under a gum tree eating leaves. A baby panda hovered close by its mother's side, masked faces furtive in all that green. They are being hunted, I thought, but it was us doing the hunting, picking through the box for the faces of the bears: a bit of nose, an eye, a paw. We went for hours without talking to each other, filling the silence with little taps on the table as we fit each piece into place. Women came by and exclaimed softly at our clever work, patting us on our shoulders with their worried hands before moving to the kitchen for coffee. I sat in the chair facing my mother's door, turning the table round as we worked on the puzzle so I didn't have to give up my view. But nothing changed as I sat there hard at work on the sky, the part of the puzzle no one else in my family liked to do except for me. I studied the pale blue pieces, letting my eyes differentiate their shapes. Together they made a crackled blue dish of a sky.

In the evenings, when the men and the rabbi came to pray, we were made to stop working on the puzzle. But I sat in my chair until my mother was led from her room, leaning like an old lady on someone's arm. "See, she's alright," my sister would say when she came out.

When the puzzle was finished my sister and I decided we would save it forever, gluing the pieces one at a time to a sheet of orange poster board we'd found downstairs in the basement. Little by little we dismantled the bears, the green trees, the sky, and put them back together for the last time, wiping off glue as it oozed up in the curved lines between the pieces. Every so often we'd peel small sheets of dried glue from our hands, comparing the fingerprints preserved there. They were different as snowflakes. It didn't matter that we were sisters. After a long time the puzzle was finished, and by then the ladies had taken their dishes and gone home, leftovers stacked in tin foil in the refrigerator, shining like my idea of Christmas when I opened the door. We took the mounted puzzle in to my mother's room and propped it on the floor where she could see it from the bed. "We made this," my sister said in a cheery voice, "for a present, for you." She nudged me and turned to go. But I couldn't speak or take my eyes off my mother.

"I can take care of you," I said. I stood in the doorway afraid to enter the room. But my mother just shook her head, *The Most Tired Woman In The World*, I thought, a side show in the circus, who would ever believe. "You'll be lonely," I told her, but my mother shook her head. My brother would stay with my father, my sister with the Steins, and I would ride the bus alone for six hours to stay with distant cousins I'd met but did not know. "Who'll feed the fish?" I said. "What will you do all day? What is wrong with you?" I yelled at her before my father came and pulled me from the room.

"Don't bother your mother," he told me.

"I won't bother her," I said, "I'll leave her alone."

"No, no, no," my mother said over and over like a baby.

The trees stand up and nothing comes of it. Hands out-stretched all the time like that, how can they bear the constant asking? I stand with my hands inside my pockets, not wishing to imitate the trees.

Rain lashed the windows of the bus, blowing us across the center line of the Interstate as if we were no more than a compact car heading due West into the storm. I bummed a cigarette off an old man who chain-smoked Old Golds and left the package laying between us like being generous was a deal he was making with God. My stomach growled and churned at the same time and I let the smoke fill me there, like the ethereal food I woke sometimes from dreams to reach for in the dark above my bed. *Just get us there*, I thought I heard the man say.

Though it was already spring, "Put some warmer things in," Mrs. Stein had insisted as I packed a plaid suitcase to go. But when she left the room I took the sweaters and the long pants out.

"When can I come home?" I asked my father on the way to the bus.

"It's up to your mother," is what he said.

Granite Bluffs rises like a thumbnail from the hand of earth, scent of blood hung so deep that even the smell of rain cannot keep it from you, or the cigarette smoke bunched around you like a veil, or will. *Give in.* The trains come there from every direction, a clutter of tracks, the stockyards in the center and the outskirts of town, men with their fierce and greedy looks buying low and feeding and selling high, steakhouses on the highway, beef barons, border town, black faces working in the plants and streets.

"This it?" Cousin David said to me when I stumbled off the bus into the rain. His wife stood behind him under a giant plaid umbrella. She had on a pale green rain coat and rubber boots that fit over the high pointy heels of her shoes.

"This is it," I told him, picking up my suitcase to go.

We got in their car. The city looked like graph paper to me, all corners in an infinite space. I'd never really been in a city before. "What do you think?" Cousin David turned and said to me.

"Okay," I said. His wife faced forward and said very little. A triangle of hair shown at the nape of her neck beneath her plastic rain bonnet. We pulled into a shiny black horseshoe of a drive. Driving on luck, I thought, as my cousin dropped us off at the door.

Briskets, hams, steaks at that table, a few canned peas on the side, a bit of salad. They didn't eat bread in their house but they did eat potatoes, a menu that suited me though I often felt too self-conscious to eat. Supper was quiet, breakfast was not. Naomi roamed the house with a dust rag in one hand, pushing a vacuum with the other, patrolling the halls, ever on the lookout for smudges and dirt. My room in their house was on the ground floor, painted lemon yellow and a high-gloss white. A double bed stood in the center of the room, swaddled in bright synthetic covers that wouldn't crumple or fold. They led me into the room, lowered the shades, closed the door. I'd never had a big bed before. I pulled back a small corner of the spread and looked down at the flowered sheets, inhaling the scent of fabric softener my mother thought too troublesome to use. You have to be there, she used to say. You have to wait till the time is right.

Twilight come and take me out, eyes closed, counting to 100, hoping each time I opened them the dream would end and I'd find myself home. Kicked my feet against the boxspring tapping out time until the phrase became an air instead of a lament, *lift me, lift me out of here*. There was a budgie in the front room but when I passed it on my way down the hall it hissed like a snake and turned its head toward the window, imagining its own thwarted flight. I ran my tongue around my lips, trying for the familiar salt of myself. But all I tasted was a sweetness there, raw as a peeled apple.

My mother stands in a fallow field, swinging her head back and forth like a clock. Why is she out in the weather like this, rain coming up from the western sky? Her coat is gray, her head is down, she is walking away from me though I see her face looking for something on the ground. I reach for her and make to rise from the bed but as I do something comes to take her up, some spiraling field of black and white holding her in its center like a pinwheel's stick, spinning and churning around her. Growing each time it takes a breath. When I look away to steady myself she recedes with the swirling thing, it is swallowing my own mother up. Harder and harder to breathe, my mother spinning away from me, her eyes held down she doesn't see me, she doesn't hear me calling her name though the swirling mass is a silence bigger than the harvest sky, bigger than the voice I cast out to her like a line to pull her back it is an unbreachable wall between us, air heavy as before a storm I cannot breathe, I cannot breathe, someone shaking me by the shoulders, slapping me firmly across the face.

There was a knock on the door and Cousin David came in, red in the face, a bit embarrassed. "Time for breakfast," he said in a cheerful voice. I'd been sitting on the side of the bed trying to will myself to stop crying. For one hour I'd sat there feeling my eyes fill up, counting to 50, counting to 100. "Are you all right in there?" he said, his head stuck like a turtle's inside the door. "Come and eat something, I know you'll feel better, your cousin's made you something nice to eat." I stood up from the bed and blotted my eyes, but nothing I did could stop my crying. I wondered what it would be like to be a person who cried all the time, in school, at the grocery store, walking down the street. *The Saddest Girl in the World*, I thought, it would just be the way I was.

Cousin David held the door for me and as I passed through pressed a five dollar bill into my hand. "Get yourself something," he said in a quiet voice.

I walked around the block three times in one day. From First Avenue to Second Street, names with no character, I thought as the cars slid by on their way downtown. Stop lights in the neighborhood, little kids holding hands as they stood on the corner to go. At home my friends and I liked to hike the cornfields in autumn, holding the strands of barbed wire open for each other, teasing the cows let loose to browse before the silage had been disked into the earth and the earth left to blow away across the state. We found an abandoned farmhouse once and went there every weekend afterward for a month, rooting through the piles of cans and old newspapers until in our minds a story emerged, a secret and tragic tale of an old woman wrongly accused of some heinous crime and exiled to a life on the prairie. When evening came we'd fill our pockets with artifacts and crawl through the underbrush home, saying nothing to our mothers when they turned the pockets of our jeans out and asked about the bottle caps and the newsprint.

Now I walked toward my cousins' house for the third and final time that day. Where was the distance I used to cover walking the fields? How had discovery come to mean the same thing as repetition?

I lay on my back looking up at the plastered ceiling, trying to commit my mother's face to memory. But the harder

I tried the more she seemed to slip away, tears eroding their shiny paths to pool in the cups of my ears.

"Time for lunch," Naomi called from outside the door.

"No thank you," I called back, trying to make my voice sound glad.

She opened the door. "Lunch in this house is at noon," she said.

"Really, I'm not hungry," I said, swiping at my face with the back of my hand.

"Then you'll sit at the table while the rest of us eat."

I sat up fast, feeling the room spin as I put my feet on the floor. "That's a girl, Grace," Naomi said.

"Do you think I could call home today? So they know I got here safe and all."

"We called your father last night," she said.

"No, my mother. After we eat. I'll pay you back for the call," I said, fingering the crisp five in the pocket of my shorts.

"Honestly, Grace," Naomi said.

"I don't feel so good," I told her, "I think I'll skip lunch." I started to cry again.

"Now look here," Naomi said, her long face hardening till I thought it would crack. "It's your mother who's unwell, not you. The last thing she needs is a spoiled child to worry about. Do you want to make her feel worse, Grace, is that what you want? Of course you don't, you're a nice young girl. So put your shoes on and wash your face. Your cousin is waiting for you and food is on the table. And stop that crying," she told me, "it won't get you anywhere in this house."

"I can't," I told her, crying harder than I had before.

"Of course you can," Naomi said.

Naomi dropped me at the public pool, saying she'd pick me up again at four. "That's plenty of time for you to get acquainted with some other children your age," she said, as if making new friends could happen like that, fast as a clock, easy and smooth as a dive. I never had to make new friends before, I'd known the same twenty kids all my life. I put my quarter in the slot and pushed my way through the gate to the locker room, turquoise beach bag slung over my shoulder in a posture I hoped looked native and relaxed. A knot of girls stood near the lockers on the left, giggling and whispering as I sat my things on a bench. "Nice bag," the tallest girl said, making the rest of them laugh again.

"Yeah?" I asked, as if I'd never noticed it before.

"You're new here, aren't you?" the tall girl said, pushing through the others to stand over me where I sat piling my things into a locker. The roof of the locker room was open to the air and the breeze blew in cool against my skin, making goose bumps rise on my pale arms. The tall girl's thighs were brown and long and smooth, and I tried not to stare at them while we talked. I looked up into her face instead.

"For awhile," I told her, "for a couple of weeks."

"You gonna sit there or are you gonna swim?" she said. I looked down at the bench.

"I guess," I told her, "I don't know."

"What do you think, you guys?" she said and all at once they were on top of me, those girls pulled me to the floor and yanked my shirt above my head while I screamed, while we all screamed, someone's nails digging into my arm while someone else tugged at the elastic of my shorts. But I'd worn my bathing suit under my clothes, and so I lay on the floor in my one piece tank trying to keep myself from shaking on the damp concrete.

"Real smart," the tall girl said and laughed. "What's your name?" she asked as I sat back up.

"I'm Grace," I said. I pulled a towel from my beach bag

and draped myself with it. The other girls had backed away, fading like paper into the washed-out white of the walls.

"That's a stupid suit," the tall girl said. "I'm Lynn," she offered, and helped me up.

I hang out bags of nesting materials for the birds in spring: scraps of quilt batting, yarns and shiny threads, jovial in their onion sacks like birthday gifts flapping up there in the trees. When I walk along the river in June, every so often I'll spot a nest trailing decoration against a clear sky.

You can judge the health of a landscape by the number of insects and birds it supports, and by this criteria my acreage is hale: bluebirds find me, blackbirds and jays, martins and warblers, or is it the mocking birds throwing me off. Come June the eyes of my neighbors say mow the grass, but I love the swarms of everything the tall grass invites, I love to watch the small bats skim its heights at dusk. I can see a long way here. In July when Mrs. Yoder sends her husband by with his riding mower, this is what I tell him, word for word: you can see your way clear to a good future with the grass so high. I cut a bunch of cosmos for his wife and give Mr. Yoder a cup of coffee and and some cake. "Take your mower home," I tell him, and sooner or later he does.

Lynn's father was Colonel Holms, we called him that when he came in the room, stiff and formal as a salute. They lived one block down and one block over from my cousins' house, in a brick-red ranch with eagles stenciled on the mailbox by Mrs. Holms. Lynn was my age and had some problem with her eyes, which stayed red and puffy as if she'd always just cried. Every week she went to a local clinic for shots, "right in the eyeball," she told me when I met her to see if I would cringe. I did. Beside her bed a table was covered with drops and creams, suggesting a regimen that made her seem older to me, more sophisticated than my friends at home with their board games and plastic horses.

Lynn's father built houses, moving his family in as the houses were finished and out again as soon as they were sold. Lynn had moved nine times in her life, sometimes down the block but often across town, leaving friends and bedrooms behind. She had lots of chores to do around the house, vacuuming and cooking and washing the clothes. "Just do it," her father said to her whenever Lynn complained. He didn't raise his voice at her but he did get mad sometimes, blacking her eye with the back of his giant hand. Then Lynn would come to my cousins' house and hide in my room till her mother came to fetch her back.

"You know better than to vex your father," her mother would whisper standing at my bedroom door, face red, arms crossed.

"I hate him," Lynn would tell her mother, hunched on the edge of my big ruffly bed.

"Don't be mean," her mother would say, "say thank-you to the Rothmans and let's go home."

"Call me," she'd hiss on her way out the door.

A grade school lay between my cousins' house and Lynn's, and we took to cutting through its yard on our way back and forth, smoking stolen cigarettes on the swing sets and slides. Neighborhood boys hung out there too, tossing gravel at each other, calling one another names. "Fuck you," they called, repetitive as parrots, curses bouncing off the brick school walls. They were pale and handsome in their slangy T-shirts, jeans torn smartly at the knees.

"Got a light?" Lynn would ask them.

"What'll you give me for it?" one of the boys would say.

Once Lynn asked for a light and the oldest boy stood up and came near her. "What'll you give me for it?" he said.

"What do you want?" said Lynn, backing up.

"What do you got?" the boy asked her, smiling. Soon another boy stood up, then another, and then there were five boys facing Lynn and smiling. I sat on the lowest swing, kicking my feet, getting restless. "Let's go," I said to her.

"Not yet," the older boy said. He picked up a rock. "What'll you give me?" he said to Lynn.

"Nothing," she told him. The boy threw the rock.

"Hey," she said, rubbing her arm where the rock had hit, leaning now against the wall.

"How about a feel?" he said to her.

"Yeah, right," she said. He threw another rock.

"Give us some," the other boys sang, coming to stand in front of my friend.

"Lynn," I said. Through the window behind her I could see the neat rows of little chairs, backs to the window, facing a board filled with cut-out birds.

"Do it," the older boy said to Lynn. He reached in and grabbed the sleeve of her shirt.

"Don't," she said. He threw a rock. Another boy reached in and grabbed her front. Three blue buttons flew off and landed glinting in the gravel, and there was Lynn's bra strap, her shoulder moonish in the falling light. The shadows had lengthened in the afternoon so now they were rangy silhouettes of themselves, Lynn and the arc of boys bigger than adults against the brick wall.

She held her shirt closed with one hand. She started to cry.

"Hey!" I yelled, standing up from the swing, but it was as if I wasn't there.

Then a bell was rung up the street. It was a mother calling the older boy to go on home and eat his supper, and soon he dropped his rocks and all the other boys went home, too. Lynn quit crying and we said goodbye and I went back to my cousins' house, looking frequently behind me in the shadows as I went.

I didn't see Lynn so much after that. "How're your eyes?" I asked her, "What have you been up to?" when I'd see her later that summer at the city pool. She wore a white bikini with black and blue flowers; with her breasts and her puffy eyes she looked much older than me I thought again, someone more tired, more filled with something I couldn't name.

"I have to go get my shots," she told me. "I'm going steady," she said, pointing to the older boy.

I wandered the dark aisles of metal shelves, fingering the greasy boxes of bolts and washers that were called auto parts in this store. Out front hung racks of chamois cloths and floor mats, novelty horns, mud flaps with naked women silhouetted across their fronts. There was fresh car spray and fuzzy dice and buffers you wore on your hands like gloves. On Saturdays Naomi came to work in the store, sitting in the office in a pink cotton dress, paying bills and making coffee and typing out business letters on the manual machine she kept covered with plastic on its own desk. I ate a glazed donut from the box she'd brought. The men who worked in my cousin's body shop came in the office to get donuts too. "Hey," they said to me, and I said hey back. One was old but one was not, he sipped coffee and glanced at me until it was time for them to go back to work. The walls of the office were made of glass, and with the door closed the people outside looked like clowns to me, gesturing, laughing, trading pieces of paper for pieces of plastic and metal. I played with the adding machine while Cousin David waited on customers behind his red formica-topped counter, adding and adding impossible columns of numbers.

"You'll wear out the ribbon," Naomi said.

I sat in the hallway of my cousins' house, twining the phone cord around my hands like a snake.

"How's Mom?" I said.

"Okay, I guess," my sister said. "But Janet Sawyer is a bitch."

"Have you seen her?" I asked.

"No way," she told me, "I avoid her like the goddamn plague."

"Really?" I said.

"Sure," my sister said, "after what she did to me I'm through with her, I'm finished."

I heard Naomi getting dinner down the hall. I pressed the telephone closer to my ear. "What'd she do to you?" I whispered.

"She talked about me behind my back, and not just once, about a million times."

"Really?" I said. "She's going out, who's she talking to?"

"Everyone," she said, "don't be an idiot Grace, Janet Sawyer is *always* out. *Way* out," she added, laughing. I could see her sitting in the Stein's front room, wearing her favorite midriff top, hair falling forward in her long face.

"I meant Mom," I said.

"Oh," my sister said. "Oh, she's all right."

I guess I must have raised my voice. "Have you seen

her much?" I wanted to know.

"God Grace, relax," my sister said, "what are you getting so hyper for? Your precious mommy is A.O.K. I gotta
go," she said, "catch ya later, 'bye."

"Bye," I said, hanging up.

Naomi's legs were weedy thin, held taut in panty hose
even in summer when the heat lapped at you damply like a
dog. Her hair was patted and sprayed into place by breakfast, except on Fridays when she wore a kerchief and went
out early to have it done. Then she came home more
upright than usual, carrying her shaved neck and high
crown of hair the way women in other countries carry baskets of food and washing on their heads.

One Friday morning when I came downstairs, Naomi
said, "Grace, how do you feel about yourself?" She didn't
often talk to me much, and I watched her now as she turned
from the sink. The collar of her housedress was buttoned
snug at her throat. She looked a little choked, I thought, as
if her words were being squeezed out of her from the bottom up, like toothpaste.

"Alright," I said.

"Do you feel you are a little... plump?" she said. "Do
you feel you're as presentable as you could be?"

I looked down at my soft, blunt hands. The idea of
being *presented* seemed odd to me; until now I'd assumed
that no one actually looked at me, as if the effect of my
watching other people the way I did naturally rendered me
somehow invisible.

"I don't know," I said.

"Well, I'd like to help you," Naomi told me in her brisk
way. "It's time you slimmed yourself down. We're going

on a diet. By the time we're through your friends back home won't even know you." She turned back to the sink. I could feel the smile and blush in her voice.

"But I *want* them to know me," is what I said.

"Oh, Grace," she said, "ever the exacting one!" She slid a grapefruit half and a glass of water in front of me. "Our first day," she told me, setting her own identical dish down. I picked up my spoon with its spiky end. I'd never eaten a grapefruit before. It seemed like something you had to acquire a taste for, like coffee or beer.

I got new clothes and a haircut and Naomi dropped me off at school the Friday before classes were supposed to start. It was a fairly new school built according to the specifications of a group of psychologists who thought the best way to combat junior high restlessness was to eliminate distractions, which translated in the building design as a general absence of windows. To make up for the loss of light, everything in the building was artificially bright, orange and royal blue lockers lining the halls. It made me nervous the further I walked inside, like entering a cave made of glossy corners. I had a new three-ring binder and an appointment with a guidance counselor named Mr. Conway, and I remember walking into his office that day, my neck all itchy from the little hairs that had fallen down the collar of my new shirt.

"Sit down," Mr. Conway said, his desk already piled with papers though school hadn't even begun. I sat. "You're Grace," he said flipping through a file, his wide tie scraping the tops of the papers like a duster when he moved. "You're new here," he said.

"Yeah," I said, "but not for long." The chair was orange

vinyl, and the back of my legs stuck to it where my skirt didn't reach.

"No," he agreed, smiling, "you'll be old hat in no time."

"No," I told him, "I mean I won't be here for long. I'm not supposed to be here."

"Oh," he said, checking my file again. "Well, here's your schedule." He handed a gridded paper across the table. "It's modular," he explained to me. "Each block represents twenty minutes. Here's Earth Science," he pointed out, "that's three mods, and P.E. and Language Arts and Social Studies. And each trimester your schedule will change."

"How long is a trimester?" I wanted to know.

"Ten weeks," Mr. Conway said.

"I won't be here," I said, taking the paper and getting up.

"I think you'll be here," he said.

"I won't be here," I said as I walked out to the curb where it was still summer, to wait.

Before the summer was over my sister came with my father to my cousins' for a visit. I spent the morning of their arrival fixing my room, putting things away in the back of the closet, making the place look as austere as possible so my father would be sorry for me and take me back home. But when they came and looked around, "very nice" was all he said, returning to the living room for a drink.

My sister was thin as January, and strong. She had breasts that pressed on the gauzy fabric of her shirt and made a curvy silhouette of her across the ground when we went outside into the sun. "Is there somewhere we can go?" she said, and I led her to a spot in the back yard where a junction of privet and olive made an alley out of view of the house. "God," she said. She took a leather pouch from her pocket, took a small pipe from in there, lit a match. She drew hard on the pipe, held her breath, let it out. She passed the pipe to me. A late mosquito buzzed my head but flew away as soon as I took the pipe to my mouth. I inhaled and held the smoke like my sister did, but my lungs couldn't sustain the blow and I burst into a cough, and I felt like I was swallowing a biting snake of fire. I handed the pipe back to her. We lay down in the grass next to each other. We closed our eyes. The noise of traffic rose off the main street like steam and I focused my ears on the rumble of trucks as they drove by, feeling the sound in my body through the earth. Then I felt the sound rise up to the sky, and it was the shudder of helicopters I was hearing, like the war on the news we watched over supper in my cousins' kitchen at night. I was sure the war had found us, my sister and me. My heart beat fast and I pressed my palms out flat as if gravity all of a sudden wasn't enough to hold me or anything else to the ground. Then, for some reason, I opened my eyes. There was my sister with her eyes closed too, and it all seemed funny to me, and I started to laugh. "Quiet," she said, laughing too despite herself. "You want them to hear us?" But I knew they were not listening for us. I knew we could do whatever we pleased and not one adult in our known world would notice.

Carrie Butheros lived in a modern house with a sloping roof and skylights, viny plants twining themselves up and around the legs of the flat, uncomfortable furniture. Carrie's mother was a former Miss America and when Carrie had slumber parties her mother made all sorts of odd things for us to eat: toasts and little pastries, recipes that came from the packages of cheese. There were five of us who came that night and we stayed in Carrie's finished basement drinking pinched brandy out of Dixie cups until the house fell quiet. Then we snuck outside into the night, giggling as we went, trying not to let the door slam closed behind us.

There were boys we knew who lived in that neighborhood, and one by one we knocked on their doors. One by one out they came, laughing at us and whispering like snakes. There was a marsh nearby and we walked there, silhouette *en masse* lit with the orange ends of cigarettes moving together down the empty street. The last boy to be picked up was the one I liked, he had long hair and listened to music full of whines and drones, though he was quiet and awkward and the same age as me. We'd met at a football game, where according to tradition boys pushed girls down a long grassy hill. Under the lights the grass shone with dew, and everywhere the shrieks of girls came louder than the voices of the announcer and the cheerleaders on the field combined. He didn't push me down the hill but he did take a liking to me, and we roamed the perimeter of the football field together, sneaking behind the bleachers to smoke pot tamped into emptied-out cigarettes. Now, when John McLaughlin put his arm around me, my body became stiff and I had to remember how to breathe. My brow began to sweat and wherever his skin and my skin touched felt cold and on fire at the same time. I shook like a paper in wind and looked straight ahead, as if the cure for my uneasiness lay somewhere ahead in the unlit night, and I could not wait to be with just my friends again, back inside my boundaried and familiar self. I waited and waited for John McLaughlin to go home. But later that night I lay awake in my sleeping bag in the basement of Carrie's house, longing for him.

There were a lot of crickets that year, the nights were full of their good-natured song. Under the streetlights, where we gathered at night after supper before bed, the sidewalks and curbs were black with them and I didn't mind the crickets, though after a while they began to annoy me with their steadiness and lack of complaint. I'd come to see cheerfulness as a kind of willful naivete. I practiced scorn in front of the mirror at night, calling up images of my brother at home, trying to make my face into something recognizable but not my own. I tried for a gaze of educated disinterest but I still looked nice when I scowled at myself, and I wasn't so sure I could change that.

If the Eskimos have so many words for snow, how can we in this region not have as many for green? The rain this year has brought it on, a bumper crop of color clean across the countryside in swathes unfurling like a runner for a bride. Not subtle, not varied, I lay in my tall grass and let the color close over me, swarms of orange butterflies in the cornflowers and Queen Anne's lace, crisp against the cloud of gravel dust hung in the air, kicked up by the last car that used my road. I didn't watch that car go by, I didn't want to see it hurrying off. Soon, they say, the Monarchs will be here and then, watch out, not a single car will pass this field and fail to notice the cottonwoods filled with their orange and black wings like a new set of leaves, passing through.

I signed up for a special Language Arts class called On Death and Dying, taught by a skinny woman named Mrs. Schneeback who cut her hair short and wore India print dresses and sandals to school. "Have you ever lost anyone close to you?" she asked on the first day, and before I raised my hand I looked around the room to see if anyone else raised theirs. No one did, so I kept mine down, but all that day my grandmother kept coming to me, shaking her bony finger in my face. "Don't lie to your teacher, Gittl," she said, "I'm dead as dead can be." I hadn't let myself think about my grandmother much. I'd been scared that if I let myself miss her a little that some hole would widen and widen in me so large I could never fill it up, and soon I'd be nothing but an empty hole from wanting my grandmother back. But there she was following me to Social Studies and gym, stockings rolled down and a Lucky hanging out the side of her mouth, and it was unmistakably her voice speaking to me, eau de lily-of-the-valley giving me a little headache in the first floor hall.

The next day in class, when Mrs. Shneeback told us to write epitaphs for a person we loved, I seized the opportunity to appease my grandmother for having lied. In seventh grade we weren't allowed to write in pencil anymore, so I took out my three-ringed notebook and a violet ball-point pen. HERE LIES MY GRANDMOTHER MASHA ESTHER RICH, I wrote. "So far so good," my grandmother said. SHE WAS THE NICEST PERSON I EVER KNEW. "Don't stretch, Gittl," my grandmother hissed in my ear. I opened my notebook to a clean page and started again. HERE LIES MY GRANDMOTHER MASHA ESTHER RICH, I wrote. But I couldn't think of what to say after that.

"What do you like about me?" my grandmother said.

"Your skin," I thought to myself, "I liked your skin."

"Skin I still got," she said, "put that down."

SHE HAD SOFT SKIN, I wrote, AND STRAIGHT HARD TEETH AND A GOOD LAUGH. My grandmother nodded, so I kept on. I LIKED THE WAY HER CEDAR CHEST MADE HER BEDROOM SMELL. I LIKED HER HANDS. I LIKED HER GOOD WIG. And soon I was listing everything I could about my grandmother, quickly, as if I had almost let her slip away. SHE TOLD GREAT STORIES, I wrote. SHE PINCHED HER CHEEKS TO MAKE THEM RED.

In thirty minutes or so, "Time's up," Mrs. Schneeback said, but I wasn't done yet, I kept writing through the first lunch bell. She walked over to my desk as the other kids in the class ran out the door, having forgotten already the topic of death. I looked up from my paper and there was Mrs. Schneeback smiling down on me with a slightly worried look. "Maybe you'd better wrap it up, Grace," she said. MASHA ESTHER RICH, I wrote again because I liked the way my hand felt to spell those words big as stars across the page. REST IN PEACE.

"I do, Dolly," my grandma said as I closed my notebook for lunch.

When Christmas break came and I got to go home, I rode the bus across the state feeling stiff as the frozen land. My father picked me up at the station and my brother came to get me, too. "You look different," my brother told me and gave me a hug. It was the first we'd ever exchanged and all of a sudden I felt old, and he'd grown tall, and muscular around the waist. My father took my bags and my brother drove the car; and though I felt changed, the places rushing by us were so deeply familiar I had to keep asking myself if I'd ever really been gone at all. There's the Clark station, I told myself, there's the Dairy Maid, pressing my thumbs into the flesh of my arms. Maybe this won't be so strange, I thought, maybe it will all be the same.

When we pulled into our driveway my heart began to beat fast, and instead of running from the car and into the house I took my time, fussing with the suitcase Naomi had given me as a Chanukah gift. "Every young lady needs good luggage," she'd said.

My mother came to stand at the door, and when I saw her face framed by the little panes of glass I couldn't help myself, I started to cry. Her eyes seemed darker and her hair was long, and instead of a housedress she'd put on pearls, dressing up for me the way she would for a stranger, someone who would judge her, instead of me.

"Why it *is* you, Grace," my father joked when he saw the tears standing out on my face, taking the suitcase from my hand.

I did wash for a neighbor with a bad back and had the pleasure of hanging someone else's sheets on the line, like flags against the lawn, describing with wind the truce of summer. She's old and proud and her son flies a plane, and last week he took me as payment in kind on a spin above the county I thought I knew so well. There it was laid out beneath us, a landscape full of lines and corners, neat as the linen I'd washed for his mom. The tassles of the corn hovered gold across the fields, and we were a small shadow skimming that landscape's unstoppable green. The higher we flew, the smaller the place became; I imagined that if we just rose higher in the air I could take my whole life in in one long look: my mother's house, my father's house, my grandma's grave; and higher still the sad town of Granite Bluffs, and back and back until the foreign land where my sister lives with her children and her dangerous men, and my brother in his city surrounded by sand, were visible as well, all of us clustered in the skirts of a swirling green. And where was I on that family map? As we came around the county, my neighbor's son pointed down, and there below us was a solitary patch of uncontrolled growth, its corners softened by the height of its grass, the house in its middle emblazened by the midday sun.   "That's your place," he yelled, though I couldn't hear him over the roar of the plane. I nodded as we circled twice, then landed in a narrow strip shaved, it seemed, from a solid mass of corn. I stepped out on the airstrip and, I don't know why, I walked out into the field while my neighbor's son set blocks in front of his airplane's wheels, readying it for a windy night. I settled myself back into the close-up world, letting the tall corn close over my head. I was sweating. I took my shoes off. I let my feet cool in the damp earth between the rows, I closed my eyes. Each stalk was human-sized and I felt safe standing still among them, a visitor in the community of corn, quiet in there save the neighborhood of bugs.

I lay on my mother's bed, watching her iron while we watched TV. The house had turned into hers while I'd been away, new curtains in the front room, furniture rearranged. She'd cleaned the closets out and, where there used to be piles of old clothes and shoes, square plastic garment bags hung in neat rows, labeled with masking tape and felt-tip pen. *Size 14, Winter* they said, *Formal Wear, Good Suits, Size 16.*

I'd put my suitcase in my old room when I got home and sat on the end of one twin bed. It seemed too small now, and meager with its pillow and plain cotton spread. She'd taken the carpet up and the oak of the floor shone bright between the little rugs she'd scattered about the room. I'd left my bag unpacked and headed for the attic stairs and sat on the day bed looking around. She hadn't gotten this far in her cleaning binge, and I eyed the dust and broken chairs gratefully, they seemed like allies to me.

Now I lay with my legs in the air, listening to *General Hospital* as it blared from the TV on my mother's big old desk. Her bed was a king-size she'd bought before my father moved out, but she slept so close to one edge she may as well have brought one of the twins in from my room, she took up that little space. It made me lonely to think of her sleeping in that big bed alone, the way she drew herself up as if she were trespassing there. "I hate you!" a woman was screaming at a man on TV. He was laughing at her, his perfect teeth glaring on the black and white set. The woman slapped him hard across the face and he was silent after that, theme music coming up as my mother licked her finger and struck it on the heated face of the iron. Without saying anything I got up to carry my suitcase from my room to hers, and when I got back she'd left a drawer in her dresser open for me, empty except for a piece of rose-scented paper. "And don't just throw things in there," she said.

That night I crawled into bed beside my mother. She said good night to me and gave me a kiss and soon after she turned on her side I heard her nasal breathing come steadily across the expanse of bed. We were as far apart as we would have been sleeping in the twin beds in my room, but here I felt much safer, as if I could monitor her dreams. I woke up the next morning believing I did, because the man from the TV came to me in my sleep. But instead of the TV woman it was my mother he was laughing at. She opened her mouth, round as a fish, but no words came out, only the shapes of words falling soundlessly at the man's feet. And then those shapes of words became reptiles writhing on the floor, and they crawled up the man's pant legs, and soon he wasn't laughing anymore. Neither was my mother; she was as afraid of the reptile words as the man was, they stood there together horrified by the words that lay between them on the floor.

When my sister came for breakfast the next day she brought a bag of her stuff over from the Steins and moved into my brother's old room. We lived together for three weeks that way, the room my sister and I had shared for so long empty and given over to whatever came along to fill it up.

My brother came early for dinner and stood in the entryway for a long time, stamping snow from his sneakers and throwing his arms around himself in a hug to get warm. My mother had roasted a turkey that day and everywhere the house was permeated with its good smell, even the attic where my sister and I sat in the afternoon, smoking pot from a wooden pipe shaped like a fist and looking at magazines.

When my brother came over we brought him upstairs too, and the three of us passed a joint around that he rolled up with the dexterous hands of a professional. It was the first time we'd ever done anything together voluntarily, and for a while we sat there, stiff in the spine, like we were at a party with people we'd never met before.

"So what do you think?" my brother finally said, breaking the silence that had come to settle like dust around our hunched shoulders.

"About what?" my sister asked, taking a hit off the joint, holding her breath.

"About Mom," he said, "do you think she's, you know, better?"

"I don't know," my sister said. "The house is sure strange, and why is she dressing up like that? It's weird," she said, "like she's out with strangers instead of home with us." She passed the joint to me, and I sucked hard at it and passed it on.

"I think she's *glad* that we're gone," my brother said, "she *likes* living here by herself, I can tell."

"No way," my sister said, "she is definitely still wacko, and I for one don't like it at all. It gives me the creeps, really *Twilight Zone*. No one else's mother is like that. I think she's crazy."

Snow had been falling all day; my eyes sought the window the way cold-blooded creatures seek ambient heat, it was crucial for me to look outside. Snow pooled in the window frames rounding out the view, and I let the voices of my brother and sister wash over me as I watched the early snow fall. The pitch of the conversation had risen to almost a quarrel, my brother arguing that our mother was fine and my sister arguing that she wasn't. I was thinking about my mother, the coolness of her hands and the things she cooked, not like Naomi's skinless chicken but weighty food that anchored me, whose tastes I could remember for a long, long time. I'd seen her taking pills standing at the counter when her back was turned. Her eyes had grown watery and old while I'd been gone, I saw the way her hand shook when she lifted a glass to drink. I pictured her without us, cleaning the house and filing her nails in front of the TV at night, talking with her friends on the phone, buying shoes, relieved not to have us there interfering with her carefully ordered life.

"She's crazy," my sister was saying.

"She doesn't care about us," my brother spat back.

"Mom's hands don't shake like that," I said. "Why do her hands shake like that," my voice catching in my throat like a bone.

They'd been leaning further and further away from each other during their conversation, and now my brother and sister pulled themselves forward again, eyes turning to take me in. But instead of the "God, Grace" I'd come to expect, they stopped arguing and turned their attention to the window, too.

"It's so quiet," is what my sister said.

My brother said, "That's so true."

Soon we went down the narrow stairs one at a time, first my brother, and in a few minutes my sister, then me. In an hour or so, when we sat down together again, we'd fallen back into our familiar selves: my sister complained of onions, my brother scraped all forms of fat from his plate, and I poured a pile of salt on mine, chewing on skin and wing tips, leaving the meat for the rest. My mother paced from counter to table and back again, smoking cigarettes, not sitting down, the way she never sat.

My father and brother lived in a trailer off a highway near my father's dealership, and one night while I was home my sister and I went for supper at their place. How compact their lives had become, how little space they inhabited, like the hermit crabs we studied in school. My father had the bedroom and the living room belonged to my brother at night, the couch unfolding into a double bed. All over the trailer lay their separate personal things, but in different areas, as if even their mess had been compartmentalized: near the sofa were my brother's shoes and bar bells, in the bathroom my father's papers and clothes. It seemed exotic and slightly dangerous to me, their life without women, and easier too, dropping their laundry off at the Wee Wash It once a week and picking it up again, folded and bleached, full of little pins and tags as if the clothes were new.

My father had changed his appearance since I'd been gone, exchanging plastic glasses for wire rims, bell-bottomed blue jeans, sideburns, a goatee. My brother wore t-shirts and gym shorts, going to the bathroom frequently to scrub his raw face and comb his long dark hair with his hands. I'd never seen them cook before, and they stood in the galley kitchen performing their tasks in silence, my father seasoning steaks, my brother fastidiously chopping carrots for a salad. The only decoration in the trailer was a row of African violet plants set in a tray on a windowsill. They looked like someone's science experiment, some of the plants getting little or no sun because of the trailer's heavy drapes, others getting too much. Some were damp and some were not, and one had a flower on it the color of Concord grapes.

"My new hobby," my father said when he saw me looking at the row of plants. He came over with a glass of water and absentmindedly sprinkled the wet plants, leaving the dry ones out. He went back to the kitchen, and I refilled the glass he'd used and watered the thirstier plants. I spilled a bit of water on the floor and stood there watching it bead up on the sculpted carpet, waiting for it to be absorbed.

"I didn't know you liked this kind of stuff, Dad," I said, remembering his indifference to my mother's shelves of dieffenbachia and purple wandering Jew.

"He doesn't," my brother chuckled, "can't you tell?"

"That's enough," my father scolded, and my sister said, "Chill out!"

"They're like this all the time, Grace," she told me. "Bitch, bitch, bitch, morning noon and night." It seemed we could talk this way in front of my father now, as if, along with his beard, he'd sprouted a new tolerance I'd only seen in TV dads.

I got dishes from the cupboard and my sister and I set the fold-out table. None of the plates matched, the flatware was flimsy, and for glasses we used jelly jars with cartoon characters racing around their sides. It wasn't that my father couldn't afford real things, he made a lot of money in the tractor trade. But everything felt on hold in that house, like the people who lived there were waiting for their real lives to begin. Until then, everything was temporary, as if at any moment they could pack their few things and fly.

My sister got out bottles of ketchup and dressing and my father played an 8-track tape of wailing, moody jazz. "This is Miles Davis," he said. "Your brother doesn't like it but he just doesn't understand this kind of music. It's full of passion and energy, don't you think, girls?"

"I think it's boring," my sister said.

"How about you, Grace?" he said, undaunted by my sister's lack of enthusiasm or the fact that my brother had pulled the phone into another room and was talking to someone in a low voice. "Let's dance," my father said, grabbing me by the waist and swirling me across the trailer floor.

"Oh gross, Dad!" my sister said, but I didn't mind. I had never danced like that before. It felt the way flying does in dreams, as if my feet were hovering a few inches off the ground and I was being propelled by the slightest current of air.

"Let me lead, Grace," my father was saying, "let my body tell yours what to do." But I couldn't read the suggestions his hand was pressing into my waist. His touch felt lighter than it ever had before, and its lack of insistence kept confusing me about which way I was supposed to go.

A bus had brought me and a bus was coming to take me away. When I went to call my father for a ride to the station, my mother stopped me as I was dialing. "I'll take

75

you," she told me. "It's only right."

I hadn't spoken to my mother in three days. When my sister told me she was moving home from the Steins I'd been struck breathless, as if someone had punched me in the stomach. I forgave my parents instantly, I was on my way to forgetting everything. But "not you, Grace," my mother had said when I asked her to call Granite Bluffs to tell them to send my things on home, to say I wasn't going back. "Not yet," she'd sighed and stroked my cheek. Instead of a comfort her touch felt like a slap, a feeling rose up in me the way my tongue had tasted for years after it had been burnt: metallic and active, the remnant of some evil wind in my mouth. Those last days, whenever I looked at my mother that feeling would take me, going for the throat like a bear gone mad, going for the gut. I wasn't not speaking to her as punishment, though I would have been right to, I told myself. It was more that that feeling was bigger than me, and I was afraid of it.

I'd sit in the attic with the door latched, smoking things, pressing my balled-up fists into myself. "Quit being a baby, Grace," my sister would yell from the other side of the door, "let me in!" I'd fall asleep with her little pipe in my hand, letting the smoke pull me down until the feeling in my stomach yanked me up again. Late at night I'd creep downstairs and get into bed beside my sleeping mother, but she was always gone before I opened my eyes the next day, I could hear her slippers scuffing across the kitchen floor.

I put my suitcase in the back of the car and I crawled in there too, making my mother drive me to the station as if I was paying her to, nothing more. "You're acting like a child, Grace," she said, "and I for one won't stand for it." She gripped the wheel with both her hands, the leather of her driving gloves shiny and smooth where they pulled across the knuckles. She lit a cigarette and I opened the window a crack, letting the street sounds in with the cold. "You'll come home when I say you can," she said. We pulled into the bus station and before she could even turn off the car, I and my suitcase were out on the sidewalk, I had my hands in my pockets and I said good-bye.

She got out of the car. I hadn't let her touch me in days, but as soon as she lay a hand on my plaid coat I started to cry, subdued at first and then a moaning so low I stopped for a moment, surprised at myself. "I'm sorry, Gracie," my mother was saying, stroking my back with a motion that felt more like a pushing away.

"What's wrong with you?" I pleaded, "you're fine, you're fine," bumping my head against her shoulder. I turned fourteen and a half exactly that day, but I didn't know what half of anything meant. A stupid age, I thought as I climbed onto the bus. An age I hate, I said.

When I was a child I read pioneer books with relish, devouring them the way I devoured the foods I loved. I envied the way those families took care of themselves, grinding wheat, amusing each other in winter when the blizzards had them trapped on the prairie. I could hear the fiddles scratching as I read, could smell the hams curing on the hooks above my head. I left that collection of books in my closet when I went away. The week I moved, my mother came through and put the books in a rummage sale pile, the Hadassah ladies placing them neatly with the other books and selling them off for a quarter. I guess my mother figured that whatever was of value I'd taken with me when I left. And, in a way, she was right, because my root cellar looks like what I remember most from those books: crates of carrots and potatoes nestled in sawdust, squash, bunches of onions, garlic braids slung over nails along the walls. I've gathered herbs and hung them in swags across my yellow kitchen, and straw flowers and statice and pearly everlastings, an image of abundance so perfect I still can't believe I made it myself.

I stood at my stove today, stirring a pot of applesauce I made from a batch of windfalls a neighbor brought by in the back of her truck, because she knew I would make something from them, the woman who makes something from nothing, mountains from molehills, memories from dust.

"Your house is amazing, Grace," she said to me, a tall woman who stands up straight ducking between rows of cut flowers.

"That's me," I said, "Amazing Grace," and we had a laugh, clearing the table of canning jars and making space for our cups of coffee.

"It must have been some farm you grew up on," my friend said, "where'd you say your parents' place was?"

"I grew up in town," I told her, pouring cream into my cup.

"But where'd you learn how to do all this?" Lydia asked me, sweeping her long arm around the jumbled room.

"Make a mess?" I grinned, "I taught myself."

When Lydia left that afternoon I washed our cups out and took the jars of sauce downstairs to shelve, and as soon as I hit the bottom step a feeling came up in me that tasted like coffee in the back of my throat, bitter and full and hot on my tongue. And, I don't know why, but I let that feeling come, in tremors that washed me like a pouring rain. *I want*, a voice inside me began to chant, *I want, I want*. Not the memories of things, but the things themselves.

I was a fish asleep in a frozen pond, dug in where the mud would keep me still, moving but slowly, breathing but slowly, waiting below the lip of ice. Wings to fins, feathers to scales, some backward evolution to keep me moving, counting off time with my tail like a clock. And how to tell, early in spring when the grayed ice melts and the pond swells to fill its banks, that the fish who rises like a sphere of air and breaks the surface hungry again for the insects gathered there, is the same fish who, long before, had gone to sleep?

Cousin David loved his car the way other people hang on to old shoes, patching them with duct tape until they're silver all around. He drove a '69 Dodge Dart and Naomi kept trying to get him to give it up. "It's not as if you can't afford better," she'd say, brushing the seat off with her handkerchief before she sat down. It was the only time I ever heard him adamant, or rather felt his refusal emanate from him like heat from a coal.

One day Cousin David got a ride to work and came home at five-thirty driving a leaf-brown Lincoln. We stood outside on the horseshoe drive, admiring the way the setting sun made the leather appointments gleam like washed hair, the white of the whitewalls unblemished by dirt. It was my birthday, but he took Naomi by the elbow and led her to the passenger's seat, leaving me standing alone as he climbed in on his side and started the new car up. It hummed like a piano string. He rolled the electric window down.

"We're going for a ride," he said.

"What about Grace?" Naomi asked, sorry to see me stranded on the pavement like that.

"She can take herself for a ride," he said, tossing me the keys to the Dodge.

I stood with my back against the body shop wall, keeping an eye on the door while I smoked in case one of my cousins came to see where I was. They never had, though I thought it couldn't hurt to watch, save Naomi's moods; they'd never even gotten mad at me, they treated me more like a house guest than like some child they had a hand in raising. I was practicing blowing smoke through my nose, watching my cousins' younger employee rip the parts from a rusty old car. We'd developed a way of talking, this guy and me, that made me feel my blood in a different way, like it was everywhere and hurried and making me tall.

"How's school?" Phil would ask me, and I would say, "It sucks."

He'd look at me through squinty eyes, smile, look back at his work.

"Pretty tough for a kid, aren't you?" he'd say.

"Well how old are *you*?" I'd ask, blowing smoke in his direction.

"Old enough," he'd tell me, and I would say, "Me, too."

But that Saturday I found myself really looking at Phil, staring at him from beneath my lowered eyes for so long I was afraid I might actually reach out and touch his skin, it seemed so smooth and dark around his neck and his face. "No really," I said, letting my voice sound like itself for once.

Phil looked over at me, a little surprised. "Nineteen," he said, in what must have been his own voice, too.

"Oh," I said. I looked up at the ceiling. There was a pattern of water stains like a thoughtful painting of clouds up there.

He put his wrench down and came over to where I was standing. He took a cigarette out of the pocket of his coveralls, he smoked Kools. "Why are you here, anyway?" he said.

"What do you mean?" I said, my real voice gone again, fled to some place I couldn't follow it to. "You tell me."

"I mean *here* here," Phil said, looking me straight in the eye. "You're bad, aren't you?" he said, smiling at me, blowing smoke through his teeth.

I didn't say anything, I looked down at the floor. He touched the back of his hand to my cheek and I felt the red flare into my face like a shot. I started to shake.

"The worst," he said, crushing his cigarette out with his heel.

"Whatever," I told him. I went inside.

I walk my rows with a bushel basket, its bottom lined with straw to keep the tomatoes from bruising beneath their own full weight. How could I believe in this, in March when I set those laughable seeds to sprout? It was the most improbable bet, that months from then they would be giving up their fruits with such ease. Like many things, the fruit of my labor is less attributable to my labor than it is to this process that, parse it as the scientists may, is still a miracle ungraspable by fact.

Last night a thunderstorm blew up around my house, a strong wind sweeping the clouds into a pile in the lowered sky. I went to the highest point on my land and laid down face up as the front rolled in. I was trying to pay attention to the moment things changed, I wanted to see what it looked like when, what used to be one way, no longer was. If we could only slow down, I told myself, if this life could be reduced to frames as in a film, we could stop the projector long enough to watch ourselves change, and make the process of that changing as seamless as a summer sky unstitched by lightning and clouds. But laying there I was taken in by the facts of the sky, the color and fullness of the clouds, the way the thunder began and the wind stopped still, the way that stillness made the trees hiss and then fall silent again, holding their breath for the rains they knew would come. The lightning came up and then in a rush the wind came up again too, blowing my hair against my face, a feeling like the precursor to rain. Then the rain began, and I knew I had lost myself, and I laughed aloud at my foolishness, and went inside to dry off.

Pressed up into a jukebox, bass line of music beating into my lower back. Some warm and yeasty breath on my neck, bit of chill at the base of the spine. To dance among strangers and drive myself home, men calling out to me in whispers that I liked. Ten o'clock Naomi said and I agreed, nodding, though as soon as I heard my cousins' talking die inside their room I went out again, rolling my small car backwards down the drive without the lights turned on, starting the engine when I hit the street. Better than any destination I liked the going away, the leaving unseen and silent in the night, the blue street, the lack of map, the moment I turned the key and pressed my foot to the gas and the driving, driving away.

I stopped being able to feel myself, bit by bit, until one night the whole length of my legs from knee to ankle were sensationless and gone. I watched the speedometer to tell how hard to press on the gas. I looked down when I came to a light and wiggled my feet. I pulled into the deserted lot of the Veteran's Hospital, turned the car off and stood beneath the mercury vapor lights, bending over to poke at the flesh of my calves. But I felt nothing when I touched myself there, only a slight resistance beneath my thumb. *The Disappearing Girl*, I named myself, cruising down the middle of Main Street, laughing.

We never went to services in Granite Bluffs except on High Holidays when even the most insubstantial believers crowded the temple pews, hungry and eager for a blare of God. Just in case. Just in case, we bought new shoes and heightened our hair and sat for a whole day quietly in dim front rooms, stomachs full of air and complaint.

My cousins' temple was a brooding place, gray and Christian-looking with its benches and stained glass. There was a choir and an organist there, but the music seemed thin and needy next to the gospel I heard on the Baptist show when I flipped round the T.V. dial on Sundays. There were big women in shining robes throwing themselves on the mercy of the Lord, and here were my cousins, stiff and nasal with their prayer books in hand, trying to follow the Hebrew with their index fingers, stumbling and embarrassed as children. True the cantor raised his voice to heaven, but his body only moved one way, bending slightly from the knees and swaying a little, like a metronome back and forth while he wailed. The women on TV were rocking too, but their hips moved and their shoulders, and their heads kept time at the ends of their solid necks. *We are meek in the shadow of the Lord*, they sang, and if that was meek then their Lord must be a powerful one indeed. Ours seemed frail and

83

cranky by comparison, and I began to tap my foot after the first half hour of prayer, trying to annoy Naomi enough that she would shoo me out to the lobby for a drink at the fountain. She did. I went across the street to a little park. There were a lot of trees but they couldn't stop the sound of the cars going by, hurried on their way to get somewhere. It was a Wednesday and I was the only kid around. A woman pushed a baby on the merry-go-round. I sat on a swing and lit a cigarette, practicing smoke rings by popping my jaw. The patent black of my good shoes stuck out against the brown of the grass, and I felt itchy and inappropriate in my nylons and checkered dress. I considered converting to the Baptist church, but I guessed you couldn't sing that way and not believe, even if you believed in the moment, the way a frightened agnostic makes deals with God. I examined my forearm. I was white, besides. The baby on the merry-go-round shrieked. "Don't scream," the mother called out, laughing, pushing the merry-go-round faster.

I drove to a state park to watch the gulls, puffing out their long wings and haggling over food on the frozen shore of a lake. *Sea*gulls, my mind would say, but this was no sea, the boundaries of the water accessible from where I sat. Little puffs of dust blew up when the wind gusted and shook my idling car. What did these birds believe, how did they come to be here? I imagined them blown, generations before, from their course en route to some coastal shore. Waking up, looking around, giving in. Fat and wrangling, some the size of young turkeys I used to see wading through the brush back home. I rubbed at the fogged up windshield with my sleeve and watched the gulls plod with their awkward feet. Was it this place making them look so dumb or had the gulls always been that way, raucous and bitter over scraps of food? I imagined not all, but maybe one of the gulls dreamed a dream of big water most nights, prodding its own breast with its beak as it slept, tides relieving it of its burden of keeping time, horizon invisible from the pebbled shore, the abundant and salty fishes.

Sitting next to me put his hand on my chest, hook of the wrist dropping to cup a breast in his palm. Leaning to kiss the nub of my ear, whispering while he did this *You like it, you know it, you do.* Put his tongue in my ear, breath marking cold paths along the way. Turned my head and closed my eyes and kissed pressed into the jukebox, his adult breath hot on my neck. He looked in my face for the first time when he felt the blunt fish of tongue inside my mouth with his own, *Some girl,* he said, and I said Yes, I said yes and pressed my hand to his face *Does it hurt you,* he asked me, *your tongue,* he said, and I said No, don't stop I said, I was breathing quietly higher this way the back of my head against my spine like a bowl I was, thought of nothing, thought of nothing at all. Later we lay on a borrowed bed, I've never done this before I said, he said, *I know* and wedged his hands between my thighs, kneading, patient, coaxing the clothes from knees and spine, I've never done this before I said again, *I know* he told me sucking my tongue, making my tongue swell to fill my mouth. I liked the character of his penis pressing against my legs, insistent I thought, I choose this I remember thinking to myself above the rhythmic lowing of his breath.

If I couldn't stay then I didn't want to go; I spent my school breaks and holidays in Granite Bluffs, doleful, livid as a bruise.

My brother majored in ethics at Kansas and my sister studied politics at Washington State, so I never lived with them again. I went with my father to visit my brother at college once, though. The land was so flat out there it made home seem punctuated and full of surprise with its frequent rills, its cattle and its farms. The further we drove the more the prairie sprawled out before us in a moving spread of wheat and grass. We sat in the Oldsmobile, my father and I, our arms hooked out the windows growing hot in the spring sun. It felt good to be moving beyond what I knew; and the further we drove the less familiar my father and I became, as if our intimacy depended on the places from which we'd come, as if my father need only be my father within a certain circumference of home and after that he was a stranger who'd brought me this far, and I was grateful to him and offered him a cigarette even though I knew, from somewhere that felt like a great distance inside me, that he was trying to quit.

We pulled into Lawrence in the afternoon, picked up my brother at his dormitory and went to a steakhouse for something to eat. The place was filled with students, piling their budget plates high at the all-you-can-eat. It was noisy after the quiet of the ride, and we had to yell to be heard inside the echoing room.

"So?" my father called, cutting into his meat. "How

goes it here in the halls of higher learning?"

It seemed clear my brother didn't want to talk with us, he kept taking little sips of cold water and holding it between his teeth before he swallowed. "It's full of racists," he said.

"Don't be ridiculous," said my father.

"Dad," I whispered under my breath, wishing for the person he'd been in the car.

"Well what's wrong with this place? It seems nice enough to me." He reached across the table and tapped my arm, signaling for a cigarette from my open pack.

"Look around," my brother whispered, knuckles gone white with the force of his grip. I looked up from my plate, but all I saw were tables of people forking pie into their mouths, eating steak.

"If you're going to make sweeping statements be prepared to back them up." My father pushed his empty plate away and a waitress came to pick it up. "You're overreacting," he said, and got up to go to the bathroom.

I cast my eyes back down again not wanting to look at my brother, who was jabbing his fork rhythmically into the palm of his hand. I looked instead at the parsley on my plate, how if I stared at it long enough the green of it filled my field of vision until everything there was green. I thought of what I could tell my brother that would make him stop stabbing his hand like that.

"I like this guy and he's black," I told him.

"*Et tu*, Miss Grace?" he said.

Here I have some wind, here a breath. Here are the trees moving and some fingers listing in the air like boats. Here is the calm of autumn, the oak leaves, the hunters in plaid shirts making their way through the littered woods. I hit a pheasant on the road today and brought it home to eat, not being able to bear the thought of that small fury gone to waste. I pulled its feathers and set them aside, blue from the tail, rust from the breast, but a gust of wind came up all of a sudden and sent the feathers flying across the bare boards of my porch. I let them go, airborne again, stewed the bird whole in a covered pot and ate the meal wrapped in a blanket outside in the late afternoon. The meat tasted faintly bruised, though pungent and hot as I took the dainty bones in my mouth and sucked each in turn, wanting to appreciate everything. Hunters we are and hunters we'll be. I scanned the darkness with patient eyes, eating that meat, enjoying it, feeling some domestic and natural variety of resignation in my bones. Early dark and all around me the empty sky, empty of stars and empty of sound, hid the shuffle of pheasants turning uneasily in their roosts.

My mother had never followed me anywhere before and now she was behind me trying to keep up, behind me when I changed lanes, speeding up to make it through the lights. It was the only time she ever came to see me in Granite Bluffs, driving the long way by herself, stopping only once for gas and a Coke, afraid she'd lose her way if she strayed too long off the road. I met her at the highway, driving slowly at first so she could follow me to our cousins' house. I watched her face in my rear view mirror, concentrating hard on keeping up with me. I sped up a little on Grandview Avenue, pulling her past the courthouse doing thirty-five. I pressed the pedal harder and still she kept up, faster and faster down the busy street. I pushed my car to sixty and left my mother stranded at a long red light, and pulled in front of a heavy truck so she couldn't see me turn. In a block or so I checked behind me for her navy blue sedan, sure she'd have caught on to me, had discovered my path on the foreign roads. But my mother and her car were nowhere in sight.

I circled around and pulled back out onto Grandview again, and there was my mother idling on the side of the road a few hundred feet from where I'd left her, nervous, her gloved hands gripping the wheel. She looked up when she saw my car, relieved and waving shyly, frightened to pull back out on the road. I lit a cigarette and studied my face in the mirror. I looked the way I had willed myself to look, smart and mean, eyes a hard sheen that made my heart beat fast.

I had a little box of mixed fittings and screws and I stood in front of the tall shelves sorting them, putting them away. Minimum wage and some time to myself, clothes after hours smelling of machine oil and smoke. I liked the dim light between the aisles, the ladder that helped me to the highest shelves, alone in a library of parts that made up the machines of men. I couldn't make one real thing but often sat fitting small pieces together, dropping my fingers randomly into boxes, connecting all the parts which, by virtue of their shapes, agreed. I'd pick up whatever object I'd made, turn it in front of my face, examine it for its possible usefulnesses, but I never found anything there. What impressed me always was the mass of the thing, potent in its ability to weigh my hand down.

Woke this morning feeling tight in my skin, like a reptile who regularly bursts from within, shedding the old as it grows. Took a walk around the place, all its abundance seeming for the first time empty to me somehow, insubstantial and wildly untalkative. A long time in front of the mirror taking an inventory I had long since stopped taking: hair to my shoulders, brown and curly in the damp air; mild blue eyes; skin that others still think remarkable, smooth and olive-toned, dotted with beauty marks, rosy patches stretched across the forehead and cheeks. An altogether European face, peasant-like and full. But I have begun to see something else there as well: a bit of puffy darkness beneath the eyes, a general pulling downwards of the flesh beneath my ears, my grandmother's face come to surface in my own like a fish breaking water with its fins. I am getting older. And I am utterly, inexcusably, alone.

Walking along the road today I was stopped by Mr. Yoder on his way home from town. He tipped his feed cap to me, a shy and mannered old man. "Have a lift?" he asked, and I said, "No, thanks, just stretching my legs."

"Stop in for a visit," he said as he pulled on by. I kept my pace until I came to his yard, clipped and swept, an old tire slung from a maple outside the kitchen door for his grandchildren to swing on when they came over. I went to the door and knocked and Mr. Yoder ushered me into his kitchen, which was dry and warm to the touch. I'd never been inside the house before. Jars lined the counters and china plates hung on hooks along the walls, and everything in there bore the shine of many hands' washing, a long life of good and serious use. Save the presence of plastic wrap and instant coffee, it could have been any other time. His wife died not long ago, a malady of the heart that took her while she slept one night. It was a merciful end and she suffered not at all. March I think it was and Mr. Yoder still got his early planting in, though of course her passing lives on in that house, waiting for him to finish his chores and come inside to face it.

I sat on a wooden chair and took my coffee with plenty of milk, listening to the small disturbances Mr. Yoder made with a spoon while stirring sugar into his own. He set a plate of sugar cookies in front of me. I took one and he said, "They're best like this," dipping a corner into his cup of coffee and popping it into his mouth before it fell. I did like he told me, and it was very good.

"That's Existentialism, Grace," Mr. Antonia said. "Right now we're talking about Buddhism, which is a different thing."

"How?" I wanted to know. I wasn't about to let him off the hook. It was the only class I liked and I made him pay for that.

"Existentialism emphasizes the isolation of the individual in an indifferent world," he said.

"But the Buddhists suffer too," I argued. It was Comparative Religions in my last year of school and, despite myself, I'd read the books.

Mr. Antonia came over to my desk. He knelt before me

and looked me in the eye, then stood up fast and walked away. When he really talked he stopped acting like a teacher and every once in a while had to remind himself where he was. "With the possibility of illumination," he said. "A compassionate existence, called what, Class?— *Enlightenment*," he went on without waiting for anyone to answer. He wrote Enlightenment on the board.

"So you're supposed to sit around feeling bad until your mind takes you somewhere else. But maybe you're still starving," I said. "Maybe the world you live in still sucks and no one seems to be doing anything about it."

"Well you're already part way there, Grace," Mr. Antonia said. "You seem to enjoy your suffering."

"Fuck you," I said, under my breath. Then the bell rang, and I closed my books and went out.

That night when I lay in bed, I pressed my thumbs and index fingers together the way I'd seen people do on TV. I tried to let my mind go blank, fall open like the pages of an empty book, but people I knew kept crowding in, filling the emptiness with themselves. I pushed them out with a sweeping motion, shook my head and lay still again, waiting for peace to come. I felt my left hip ache, then a little throbbing in my temples began, growing in strength till someone pushed through again, my mother filling up whatever room I was able to make. She had her lipstick on and a business suit, and a briefcase underneath her arm because while I'd been away she'd gone back to school, in four years taken a law degree and gotten a job in a firm near our town. She looked happy and smart in my mind and I hated her. And where I'd wanted only space to be I let that hate fill me until I fell asleep, and dreamed of nothing until I woke up.

"Turn left," my grandmother said and so I did. "These people are not your people," she said, and though I didn't know who she was talking about I knew what she meant: no one seemed to belong to me. "Turn right," she said. "Put gas in the car, fill it up," so I pulled into the Payless Station and did as I was told, bought a carton of Luckys and drove away. I had some money in my pocket and a charge card for gas that Cousin David had given me one Sunday after I hadn't come home to his house to sleep. "Just in case," he'd told me, and I'd said, "Yes."

"Take the highway," my grandmother said, I felt her breath tickling my ear she was so close, so clear, so warm behind my neck.

"Which one?" I asked, but she didn't seem to care.

"The longest one," she told me, "whichever will take you the furthest away."

"But I can't just go," I said.

"Why not?" she asked me, "what do you do here, Dolly, you drink, you let those men touch you, they're not even boys for Godssake," she said. "Now get on the highway," she told me, "and go."

"But there's the cousins," I said.

"*Feh*," my grandmother told me and spit on the floor of the car.

I turned left off of Upland, pointing the nose of the car out onto the highway. A place in my body had opened up while she talked; it was as if some strong wind was passing through me now, the cold from it catching in my throat as it blew. I was hollow. I was lonely. I started to cry from that hole in me, some bitter, confused shock rising up, more dense than steam but as endless, abundant as water. I couldn't see to drive anymore, so I pulled to the shoulder of the Interstate and stopped. Equations began making themselves inside of me, every one of them unsolvable: If my grandmother hadn't died. If I hadn't lain in my bed at night cursing her beneath my breath. If I hadn't clung to my mother's neck, if I hadn't failed her. If I hadn't failed. If my mother were here, then I wouldn't be feeling this. If I could touch her, right now, this wouldn't be happening to me. I lay with my whole body draped over the steering column feeling an unassailable weight, and cried.

After a long time I lifted my head. My mother was gone and my grandmother was dead; I knew this, and as soon as I knew it I couldn't smell either of them anymore or hear my grandmother's voice telling me what to do. The smell of cold and car exhaust hit me full in the face, and it was like a tonic; I pulled into the lane and drove on. I lit a cigarette and drove. I turned the radio on, I turned it off, and drove. I was tired and wide awake at the same time, but the further I went the more determined I became though I had no idea where I was headed that night. No moon shone but the sky was clear; the only light to see by was the light I made hurling myself down the road. And then out of nowhere a pair of eyes met mine and I struck them head on in the dark. All I remember from that moment on was the sound of the car engine wanting, trying to keep moving ahead, while the actual car stood still.

I made a soup of carrots and squash today and took some over to Mr. Yoder for lunch. He'd never eaten curry before but he was game to try.

"Tastes of the sun," he said when he ate, pushing his bowl out for more.

I hit the calf going sixty-five and never saw that animal again. The fence had been damaged for weeks, the state trooper said, the old man's cattle nearly killed a woman before, a visiting nurse who was thrown from her car and applied a tourniquet to her own leg till someone stopped to help. "It wasn't your fault," the trooper patted my arm, "it wasn't your fault at all."

I stood beneath the fluorescent lights of the emergency room, holding myself upright against the corner of a table. "I'm fine," I kept saying when someone came in. I wouldn't let them help me or lift me onto a table, I was too heavy, I was fine, I said. I had a bag of pot stuffed in my sock, and as soon as the doctor had patched my head I went to the bathroom and took it out. I meant to flush it down the toilet but I took out my little pipe instead, filled it, smoked it, filled it again, keeping a cigarette lit to mask the smell. I got rid of the rest then, washed my mouth and my face and went back out into the blaring light. David stood in the corner whispering with the highway patrolman, shaking his head and looking down at the ground. "Look at you," Naomi said, brushing the hair off my face.

"I'm fine, really," I told her, moving my head away from her hand. We got in the car and I felt like I did the first time they ever came to pick me up, strangers bound for a life together we hadn't, any of us, chosen.

"Aren't you lucky," David said. "If you hadn't been going the speed limit you'd be dead or worse." He never wore one before but now he pulled his seat belt across his lap.

"What's worse than dead?" I asked.

"Go and ask that cow," he said, and we had a little laugh. I'd gotten forty-five minutes from Granite Bluffs and five miles short of the state line, an irony I thought about and shook my head at as we drove.

Naomi was silent the whole way back, and I thought she'd fallen asleep bolt upright in her seat. But as soon as we pulled in the drive and David got out to put the garage door up, she spoke to me without turning around.

"And just where is it you think you were going, Grace?" she said.

December of that year I graduated from school, six months early and ranked high in my class though I'd tried my hardest to fail.

"What's out there for you, Grace?" Mr. Antonia asked.

All I'd thought of up to that day was getting out, getting out, an imperative which blocked the way for any other. "Nothing boring, I hope," I said.

It was early in the period and not everyone had come into the room yet. "What doesn't bore you?" he said.

I looked at him through my foggy eyes. I'd smoked a joint before coming inside, expecting the day to be one long exhale, nothing more. "Nothing," I told him. "I don't know."

He grabbed my chin and held it then, pinched it in his big hand, let it go. He shook his head slowly. "Well I hope you figure it out soon," he said.

At night when I went out with my friends I'd stand near the bathrooms sipping shots of Black Velvet and watching the black men move. I liked the way they used their hips, the way they made their necks move so slightly from side to side. The men closed their eyes while they danced but the black girls shot us looks from the floor, what few black girls came into that bar. Mostly it was black men with white girls and white girls waiting by the bar to dance. I hung back where the light was dim, pouring shots from a fifth I carried in my bag. I feigned mystery, I feigned dark and intense, I knew what smooth skin felt like to touch and thought about it while I watched the men dance.

Near last call I'd start eyeing the door, and sometimes at two in Phil would come. I'd wait where I was and watch him saunter through the crowd shaking hands with his friends. Then maybe he'd find me, maybe he'd touch me, maybe he'd take me outside in his car. He'd hold me. He'd kiss me. He'd tell me I was good. "Baby," he'd whisper, "I like how you feel." The problem was I couldn't remember when my last blood had come; I felt it was longer ago than it should have been. Now I checked and checked myself, excusing myself from the table midway through a meal. "What's wrong with you?" Naomi asked, and I said, "Nothing," as I left the room. I'd stick my finger inside myself, probing, trying to coax my body to bleed, but it would not. I spent those days in a dreamlike state, calm as a church. I'd go to the bar and watch the dance, following one man or another onto the floor, rocking back and forth from the hips like him, nodding like him, closing my eyes. I'd go in the bathroom, drink a shot, and press my heels into the floor, finger inside me searching for blood. True or false it didn't signify a baby to me, I never once thought of it as that. It only meant the end of me as I knew myself, an outcome I alternately courted and feared.

When my period finally came it fell from my body like rain. I lay in bed for a couple of days, chilly and cramped, unable to remember what I'd been so anxious for.

Naomi planned a special dinner for me before I left Granite Bluffs. But instead of the meal I thought she'd cook, they decided to take me out to eat. We didn't do that much, my cousins and I, Naomi's grip could only reach so far and it made her uneasy not to know what was going in us as food. She insisted on visiting the kitchens of the few places we went, a requirement so humiliating Cousin David and I rarely suggested going out. Now we were headed for the Meadowlark Club, quiet in the car in our dress-up clothes.

A relish tray appeared as soon as we sat down, a woman in a black uniform brought it over to us. Then hot rolls and butter after we ordered our steaks, and a basket of crisp onion rings the place was supposed to be famous for. It was the most food I'd ever seen on a table at which my cousins also sat; they kept looking over at me expectantly in between bites, pushing things my way, especially Naomi, who looked for the first time as if my pleasure meant something to her.

"Well, you must be happy to see me go," I said, trying to amuse them and break the grip of their intention on me.

David smiled, but Naomi's face crumpled as if I'd given her a slap. "What a horrible thing to say, Grace!" she cried. "I may not have been the easiest person to live with, but neither were you! Not that I'm complaining, you've become like a daughter to me and I've learned to take the good with the bad, haven't I, David?" she asked her husband.

He was wiping his mouth with his napkin, his face flushed and moist as if he had a fever rising up from the neck of his best white shirt. "Of course you have," he murmured, "of course."

I laid my fork down and stared at my plate. Martini glasses floated by us on trays, olives bobbing along the rims like boats. Over the Muzak a tape of meadowlark song was playing and it mixed in oddly with the clink of china and silver, as if the inside and the outside had become one place while I wasn't looking, the animal kingdom peopled with ladies in fur stoles and men in suits. Like a zoo, I thought.

The waitress came and laid our steaks in front of us, little plastic tags in red and pink signifying rare and well-done. I felt like an animal too, but rough and hungry and untame, nothing like the others. I picked up my knife and fork, unable, for a moment, to remember what they were for. I looked up from my plate and into the faces of the people I had lived with for a long time now. They still looked like strangers to me.

"I was only kidding," I said.

My father had moved to a big old house, one he renovated from the bottom up and lived in with his girlfriend who was a practical nurse in town. He'd sent me polaroids of the place while I'd been away, but they'd never made any sense to me: a swath of dormant forsythia, an unmade bed on a sleeping porch. Now I was sitting in the living room, stereo equipment lining the walls and a huge TV that showed a football game, though no sound was coming out. "Well?" my father was saying, "what do you think?"

"It's great, Dad," I told him, though I wasn't quite sure what he was referring to. His girlfriend came in and handed me a glass of ginger ale, diet, with a napkin underneath. "Thanks," I said, and sat up straight. She was as tall as my father and her name was Lavonne. She wore her black hair pulled back tight in a bun and she looked like a ballet dancer to me, stern around the eyes with extremely white teeth. She was black, I guessed, though her skin was no darker than mine got in the summer. How strange that people could hate her and not me, and her so beautiful, I thought, staring.

"How was your trip, Grace?" she said, and I looked

away from her face when she talked.

"Fine," I told her. "I like driving."

"You really do, don't you?" my father said, as if I'd revealed some part of myself he'd never fully appreciated before. "Slaughter any livestock on your way home?"

"Oh leave the girl alone, Stan." Lavonne punched my father in the shoulder.

I began to feel a little dizzy sitting there on the couch. I kept looking from my father to the woman he was with, trying not to imagine them sleeping together but unable not to. She seemed so unmother-like to me, which meant, of course, so unlike my mother. Their house looked nothing like ours ever had. As far as I knew, my father had never chosen anything in our house, nor did he ever seem particularly interested. Now he'd taken to collecting modern art; his new walls were heavy with paper cutouts and paintings in lucite frames. This is my father's taste, I thought. I would never have guessed this was what he liked. I looked at my father's face again. I have his mouth, I thought, but other than that he seemed completely unrelated to me.

The prairie wind calls out the names of our towns: *Justice, Justice, So Long, So Long.*

My mother stayed put in the old house, commuting to town every day to represent old people and children's rights. She favored the underdog and stayed up nights working, fueled by an immutable fury and an unimpeachable sense of what was right. She had changed so much since I'd moved away, crisp now in her business suits, the sound of her briefcase snapping closed as I woke up. As for the house, it was spare and white, with angular furniture and track lighting and carpets pale against the polished wood floors. She had a cleaning girl come weekly who was not much older than me, who brought her kids with her and pulled sandwiches from a carpet bag for their lunch.

I drove my mother to work in the morning and spent my first days back driving around in town. I ran errands for her, picked up her dry cleaning, shopped for food. I parked and walked the university campus, wandering among the students with their book bags and clumps of friends. I may have looked it but I didn't feel like one of them, I was unattached, mystified and frightened by their lives. I tried to picture them living on their own in those little rooms, someone you didn't know sharing the bed across the way.

I stopped for my mother again at five and went into her office to pick her up.

"And you must be Grace," the secretaries said. "Your mother talks about you all the time, living out there by yourself and all."

"Not by herself," my mother corrected them, as if Granite Bluffs had been a move I'd vied for and to which she had only grudgingly agreed, setting strict rules for my living away. She closed her briefcase, locked it, said good night.

My mother cooked supper and we ate together at her new table, which was small and round. The table we used to eat at was huge, my brother's handwriting scratched into the almond formica. It was the surest way to make a child behave, I thought, change the furniture on her, get rid of the familiar smells. I sipped ice water from a smoky tumbler and folded my napkin when I was through.

"What are your plans, Grace?" my mother said, pushing her plate away.

"As if I had a choice."

"Of course you have a choice," she said, as if she was surprised at my asking, as if it had always been so. She lit a cigarette and offered me one from her pack.

"You mean I could move back in here?" I asked.

"If you want to," she said, dropping ash onto her plate.

"Then I want to."

"Good," she said, "I have a catalogue for you." She reached for her briefcase and undid the clasps.

"For what?" I asked.

"For school," she said.

"But I just got *out* of school." I lit my cigarette and scratched my head.

She sat back in her seat, set her mouth, looked at me hard. "You're not a kid anymore, Grace. If you want to live here, with me, then you'll be doing something for yourself. You'll not be sitting around here watching television and smoking dope all day. You think I don't know what goes on?" she said, arching an eyebrow, a little pleased with herself.

I *did* think that. "I'll get a job," I told her.

"You'll go to school," she said.

For some reason words had begun coming into my mind at random, unbidden. It had started on my long drive home: I'd be passing a trailer on the interstate and I'd think *gullible*, then a few miles on it was *ingratiating*, *perspicacity*, words I didn't know the meanings of let alone had ever used in conversation. The word *scarcity* came to me now, and I took the entire pack of cigarettes my mother was offering me, put them in the breast pocket of my shirt, and went upstairs to the attic before she could say another word. I laid the cigarettes out next to me on the daybed and lit a match to one. I watched the flame as it travelled the short way to my fingers and when it burned my flesh I let it drop to the bed. It made a black hole in the synthetic blanket, which was a murky green.

I lay in the attic that night looking out the window at the stars. The night was cold and the sky was clear, and I could not hear my mother pouring herself a cup of coffee, settling in at her desk to work. I listened for her feet shuffling across the floor in the slippers she'd always worn, fuzzy ones in pink or blue fur that matted down to a sheeny pelt after the first few days she owned them. But she had taken to going around in her stocking feet while I was gone, and I could no longer chart her progress from table to stove the way I used to, waiting to fall asleep at night. She was down there in silence and she liked it that way, the right angles of her counters and the gray of her couch. "Close that cabinet!" she had snapped when I was putting the dishes away after supper, as if the smallest thing left unattended in her life would send her careening backward to a time she was glad had passed.

And so I was alone in the house with my mother to myself, gazing out the window with the moon coming through. But what I'd longed for in my years away didn't seem to exist anymore, like the fossilized snails I'd collected as a kid, imagining our yard as the ocean floor it must have been once. *You have what you want, you have what you want,* I tried to convince myself in order to fall asleep. Still I could not stop listening for my mother's footsteps at night, nor did I ever sleep easily in that house again.

Keeping my friend Lydia on the front porch is like trying to keep wind out of a leaky barn: you can't. "What are you always scribbling on?" she said as she blew through my door, landing at the kitchen table, waiting for a cup of tea.

"Oh nothing," I said, but I could feel my evasions wearing thin. She tapped a red fingernail against the table with a patient, annoying smile on her face. I put the kettle on, took my notebook from the table and put it in its drawer by the stove.

"You're such a mystery, Grace," she said.

When the water was hot I got up to fix the tea, and when I picked up the kettle saw my face reflected there, stretched and spread thin across the shining steel. It was hard to believe I was mysterious to anyone; it seemed like everything I'd ever done or seen was right there on my surface for everyone to see. "Maybe you just don't look hard enough, Lydia," I said. My glasses were crooked and when I reached up to right them some of the boiling water poured out onto the floor, a bit of it catching my bare foot on the way down. It didn't hurt much but I let out a yelp, and with Lydia there watching I sank to the floor in tears. I hadn't cried in a long, long time, and once I'd begun I didn't seem to be able to stop. Lydia, unfazed, sat right down with me. She put her arms around me and I put my head on her big shoulder and sobbed. "Tell me how it hurts you, sugar," she said, trying to look at my foot and hold me at the same time.

"I'm okay," I tried to tell her, choking and coughing like a stopped exhaust. In a minute or two I got myself free of her and stood at the counter looking down at my foot. Lydia was still on the floor and I offered a hand to help her up.

"You'll have a hell of a blister," she said, taking my hand and holding it as if we had come to some agreement.

I waited for my mother to take her catalogues back, to beg me to stay with her just as I was; but that's not what she did when I threatened to move across country to my sister's state.

"It's your decision," was all she said, bought me a membership to AAA and helped me pack my things.

Following Interstate 80 the country changed from rolling to flat, hilly again then mountainous so by the time I got to Washington I felt I'd been through something, as if I'd aged. Nebraska was an endless plateau of cows, Montana with its female contours, and all along the way the country music, the worst full of whining and the best all attitude and lament. I drove straight through, stopping only to eat and sleep, avoiding truck stops and the leers of lonesome and hurried men, choosing instead to drive into some small town and park in a neighborhood until the light came. I liked sleeping near houses like that, I could fall asleep imagining the dreams of children. Somewhere along the way I'd come to believe that I was not one anymore, a child, each mile of the drive ripening me like a green fruit. I ate meals in diners, ordering foods I'd never tasted before: scrapple, buffalo meat, sausage gravy, grits. There was a stretch of road in Wyoming so littered with dead rabbits I counted one every tenth of a mile. I had a leaky tire near Coeur d'Alene and had to stop early one afternoon, finding a garage just before the tire went completely flat. The mechanic was a young man with friendly eyes and bad teeth, and I liked the familiar smells of oil and smoke and sweat on his clothes. "Where you headed?" he asked me, raising my car on a lift.

"Washington State," I said, "why?"

"Just asking," he told me, "a girl like you, so far away from home and all. I bet your daddy doesn't know where you are."

"Just fix the tire," I told him, and laughed. He didn't charge me anything and afterward we went to a bar where we bought each other shots of scotch until dark.

"You drink good," he said, draping his arm around me, kissing me on the mouth. I liked the way his teeth felt on my tongue, rough and dangerous, like I could cut myself there. "I'll rub your back," he told me, "you're tired from the drive." I woke the next morning curled into a corner of a double bed, the mechanic sprawled across the mattress. I was sore between the legs and sick in the pit of my stomach, and I was out of there before he next twitched in his sleep. I left ten bucks on the night stand thinking to pay him for the work he'd done, then took the money back and went out. The day was gray and even though I was hungry I pressed on through, wanting to get where I was going and soon.

The next day I pulled into my sister's town. I drove until I came to the water, a rocky beach littered with barnacles and wrack. Boats lined a little pier and I went into a fish house and asked to use the phone. "I'm here," I said when she answered the phone.

But the person on the other end was not my sister. "She's gone for the weekend," her roommate said, "but you can leave her a message."

Jays at the feeder, the insatiable squirrels. Goldfinches faded in winter to blend into the sky, plain siblings to the cardinals' year-round red.

I loved the smooth orange bark of the madrones and their glossy leaves, the way the rain kept the green of things clean and sharp against the unremarkable sky. I found a cottage in New Hope for one hundred dollars a month surrounded by blackberry and Italian plums, with a view of the water when I walked outside and a tiny electric range on which I learned I could cook. I decorated my one room with trinkets I'd brought from the attic at home: a cotton bedspread, two of my grandmother's china cups, a carnival glass bowl full of kernels of dried corn. The rest of the things in there I made or found: a book shelf, some houseplants, a fabric runner for the table. I chose things specifically to catch the sun when it came, crystals off a chandelier, glass-bead edging for the windows, glossy white paint for the concrete-block walls. When the day was fine the mountains came out around me like those flowers that bloom in the desert only briefly, after the one long rain of the year.

My sister came by for coffee unannounced, and usually I didn't mind, I liked the way she burst through the door mid-sentence and told me stories about her friends. It gave me a life outside the house without my ever having to leave, a way of being I took naturally to. She lived with her lover who dwarfed her in age by at least ten years, a cynical, artistic man who worked as secretary at a public school and wrote novels at night on the sly. She was active in political groups, staging actions at the state capital, teaching immigrant women to talk English and speak up. I cooked jam, I dried plums. I talked to my mother every Saturday at eight, though for the first month or so we spoke nearly every day, as if the distance between us melted our obdurate postures and there was nothing left for us to do now but weep and long for each other over the phone. I got a job serving Chinese food at a restaurant in town and in spring enrolled in an organic farming course at the local state college, where, plunging my hands into the friable earth, I believed I'd found what I was meant to do, an activity requiring nothing but my willingness to bend, to kneel.

My mother flew in for a long visit my second season there and my sister came daily to eat and talk, slurping my mother's chicken soup loudly and belching when she was done.

"No man will ever take you out for a nice dinner if you belch like that!" my mother cried, the same objection she'd been raising since my sister was a child, ignoring the fact that men adored my sister, no matter what sounds she made. Often I left them in the cottage to talk, visiting for respite my fertile beds, pulling beets for the borscht my mother had promised to make us for supper. She left her briefcase home and became, in that strange land, our mother again, and I could not believe my good luck to have her back.

It was almost too much at once, my mother and me. We spent our days easily together and every so often she let me serve her, making her cups of weak coffee at night. She couldn't drive a stick shift so I drove into town for the paper each morning, bringing home glazed donuts in a waxy sack. She did the crossword puzzle while I went outside to mulch or weed, and she and my sister came to eat at the Chinese restaurant at night, ordering potstickers and laughing when

I brought their food. "You a waitress," my mother would say, "the least coordinated of my children lifting trays above her head!"

My mother had a married lover who came to see her at my house for a weekend. He taught law at a university and loved the out-of-doors, and my mother planned for them to sleep like teenagers in a tent in the backyard when he came.

"Sidney!" she squealed when he walked in the door, blushing on the edge of her seat, asking questions. He sat, crossed his legs, uncrossed them, answered her enthusiasm with news of himself. Not once did he ask her about her life, nor did she ever offer. She just sat there, embarrassed and pleased, the pitch of her voice noticeably higher than before he'd arrived, all her fire and stubborn intelligence vanished like a flower closed up for the night.

"Would you like a cold drink?" she asked him, and he said, "Sure." We took chairs outside and sat in the garden next to a sprawl of zucchini with which I'd lined the path.

"This is quite a place here, Grace," he said, tapping the ash from his pipe out into the dirt.

"Yes," I said, "thanks."

"And your mother," he told me. "Quite a woman, she is."

I just sat there not knowing what to say, hoping my mother's friend wouldn't notice the ruddy color in my face, or the fruits which lay beneath the squash leaves like a big woman's breasts. *You don't know her*, is what I thought. *You couldn't see her if she stood in front of you naked, demanding, showing you who she was.*

"Grace, please, don't bore the man," my mother came out saying with a tray full of iced tea. She'd put on fresh lipstick, I could smell her powder as she served the man first. I noticed a weed. I pulled it out. I imagined I was fated to always be mad at my mother.

My sister sat at my table and rolled a joint. She lit it, passed it to me, I smoked, passed it on. My mother took some, held it in, passed it on, and so forth in silence until we couldn't hold the burning paper in our hands anymore. We looked away from each other, unsure and twitching lightly in our chairs. I'd washed my windows the day before and all of a sudden a bird began hurling itself into the clean glass thinking it open, thinking it empty. Finally, exhausted, it fell to the ground, and we went outside to check it out. We stood before it, the three of us, until my sister knelt and cupped the bird in her hands. It was a chickadee, simple, black and white stripes across its head. "It's still alive," she said. She passed the bird into my hands. I could feel its heart beating in my open palms. My mother cupped her hands and I passed the bird to her, and we watched her stand there as we had, feeling the bird's life like a message, like a code. We found a box and laid the bird inside, checking every half hour to see if it had come to. As the day went on we checked less often, until by evening we'd forgotten the bird entirely and went to sleep without a thought.

The next morning I got up early and found my mother standing by the door in her robe holding an empty box.

"Our bird is gone," she said.

I've taken to watching television with Mr. Yoder on Saturday nights, cooking supper for us over there and watching the news together at five. For their fiftieth anniversary their children pitched in and bought them a dish, and for months after Mrs. Yoder died the old man sat

110

flipping through stations until it was late enough to sleep. He never really watches anything except the news, preferring the radio for farm reports and choir music on Sunday mornings. He likes things that are funny but never could take to laughing alone, he says, it makes him feel a little crazy. He doesn't care for new shows. He doesn't like *Green Acres* because it makes farm people look ignorant, nor does he care for anything mean-spirited or ugly. Usually that means re-runs of *Carol Burnett* at seven, and before that the national news, and before that anything local.

I was making a chicken pie that night and could hear the voice of the newscaster murmuring through the open door. Mr. Yoder liked to keep me up on things while I was in there cooking. "Housing starts down," he called in a somber tone, because the news was a solemn occasion and he felt it his duty to honor that, then, "Grace, we've gone to war."

I came out of the kitchen drying my hands on my pants. On the screen was a reporter dressed in khaki and flak, lights from missiles illuminating the city around him in flashes. "What is happening?" I said. But even as I said the words I knew what was going on. While I stood in the kitchen cooking chicken for Mr. Yoder, another man on the television was standing on the roof of a hotel in Jerusalem, waiting for the bombs he'd been told would come.

"Over what?" I said, shaking my head.

"Over what's right," Mr. Yoder said back, neither of us looking away from the set.

"Those are real people there," I told him.

"I've been to war, Grace," he said, looking me in the eye. I went back in the kitchen and fixed us both plates. "This is good," Mr. Yoder said. It was, I knew, taking one bite and then another, burning, slightly, the roof of my mouth. I thought of my brother with his wife and his one young son. It was early in the morning there and probably he'd been up all night, sitting in a chair with the lights turned off, praying to God not to target his house.

"My brother lives there," I said. Mr. Yoder laid down his fork.

I met my friend Rena my first week at school. She was weeding a little patch of plants she had hidden in the woods and I was walking a bit away from the class, trying to tame my self-consciousness and relax. She stood up when she heard me come. "My experiment," she said and laughed out loud. The plants she'd been tending were stocky and full of buds, little hairs standing on end and catching the light like jewels. "*Cannibus Indica,* dwarf variety," she said, "care to participate in my research?"

Though she was taking some courses at the organic farm, Rena was an art major learning how to weld. She spent long hours in her studio at school, and I took to sitting with her while she worked, reading aloud, talking, stitching pieces for quilts. Rena was Italian from upstate New York, and she needed pasta the way I needed chicken soup: regularly, in quantity, without any interference. We often sat in her kitchen, Rena pouring olive oil from a gallon can onto my plate.

Rena's lover was a biology major who fasted once a month on carrot juice until her skin turned orange. If she minded me around then she didn't say; I brought her fresh vegetables and we talked about plants, though theory was never my strong suit and practice was never hers. I met their friends and they took me in, not a man among them. Most of them were from the East, and I didn't mind being the anomaly among them, odd girl out, answering questions about the Midwest, a place exotic as an island to them. "There are *Jews* there?" they said and I said yes, showing pictures of my family, and farms, and our house which even to me looked rustic and American. Their perception of us was never very accurate, but I let them think what they wanted. I liked the myth they saw. For the first time in my life I was a person with a past and I could make of it what I wanted, rendering it harmless and benign as snow.

Rena's friends used language that had embarrassed me as a child, announced their periods out loud and referred to themselves as women, but they weren't much older than me. They were largely vegetarian and worked for various political causes, and while we learned to cook the appropriate lentil loaves for potluck suppers, Rena and I snuck off to the Masthead Diner late most nights and told Helen Keller jokes over burgers.

There was an infestation of carrot rust in the root cellar at school, and the faculty had decided on their own to spray the place with fungicide at night when we weren't around. I'd grown a vocal intolerance to hypocrisy by then, keyed up and vibrant as a tuning fork when struck; and for that reason a handful of students, including myself, boycotted the program. We let our gardens run to weeds, the round and quarter-round beds a group of us had made jumping their boundaries like rabbits unpenned. I couldn't bear to see it all ruined like that; the quarter break came, and I never got around to re-registering. I sat in my house and brooded instead, humorless and sullen as a weed.

"I swear, Grace," Rena ranted at me when she came over to visit, "I'm gonna paint a vagina on your door. It's like a womb in there," she said, "but sooner or later you've got to come out." And, with Rena cajoling, teasing me on like that, how could I resist, I did.

She swore she'd only be gone for a month, but when my sister left town she moved all her boxes to my place and gave up her room in her house. She left her lover for being maudlin and depressed, joined a coalition of American leftists, and was headed for Nicaragua on a Peace Brigade to pick coffee in the mountains, and cotton, and grapes. She'd never seemed interested in farm work before, but I knew that was the least part of her going. It's as if my sister's spirit is programmed to itch, and she was itching that year and looking for a fight.

"They could use your skills, too, Grace," she said. "Come with us why don't you? What have you got here?"

We looked around my place. It seemed so obvious to me.

"I can't," I told her. "It's not for me."

Her hair had grown long and thick and dark, and her deep eyes flashed though the day was gray. Along with her good looks she'd inherited our mother's sense of outrage and fairness. "Well, I personally can't stand doing nothing," she said. She got up from the table and washed out our cups, unable to sit still for even a moment.

"I hope Nicaragua can stand you," I said.

"Shut up, Grace," she told me and snapped me with a towel. A person ready to fly, I thought. A woman equal to a war.

I was awake as a flower then, rose of sharon, hollyhock, pride-of-the-mountain. I built my first greenhouse out of saplings that year, unfurling the wide rolls of heavy plastic to flutter in the breeze like flags. Rena helped, treating the project as sculpture and making artful angles with the trees, leaving the responsibility of the site to me. It faced south by southeast to get the earliest sun, and by the evening of the fourth day it was done. We climbed the ladder and

114

straddled the roof, watching the sun go down over the dark water. We made supper and took our bowls up there, eating soup and looking out at the stars. Gradually the sky began to undulate and shift, rays of color moving outward from an ill-defined source. I'd never seen anything like it before, that pulsing, hushing green. I took Rena's arm, I didn't plan to but I started stroking it gently in the rhythm of the lights. She put her hand out and touched my breast, and every part of my skin came about to face the direction of that touch, and my organs, and all of my bones as well. I'd never kissed a girl before but once I did I didn't want to stop. It was like the sky, a revelation to me.

"Grace," my mother said, "what are your plans for Christmas?"

It was a conversation we had every year, would I come or would I not. I hated to travel to the Midwest in winter. The thought of getting trapped there, snowed in for some unknown period of time, had come to feel like a threat to me, the place I'd loved and had never wanted to leave a sinkhole that could swallow me up if I stayed too long. Though I'd lived there most of my life, now it took my body days to recover from the shock of that unchecked cold. Besides, I liked the life I led and I hated being away from it, Rena, my friends, the garden. I'd quit my job at the restaurant and sold vegetables and flowers to the co-op instead, and quilts, and any other things I made that seemed nice enough to sell. For the first time it seemed to really *need* me, my life, more than my mother did for a holiday we didn't celebrate anyway.

"I don't know, Ma," I said, letting my voice trail off. I ran my fingers through a bowl of uncooked rice I kept on the table. I'd given up smoking and I liked the way the grains felt against my skin, passifying the nerve endings, keeping them busy.

I expected her to get angry like she usually did, but instead her voice turned ironic on the other end. "Isn't it funny," she said, "you used to beg me to come home for a week, now I can't get you to save my life."

"Well if it came to *that*," I said.

"It's come to that," she said. I choked on my breath and began to cough. I started to sweat and the sweat chilled my skin, and I sat there shivering with the phone pressed against my face.

"What do you mean?" I said when I could speak again.

"It seems I'm sick, Grace," she said in that same ironic voice, a bit of wonder there like something phenomenal had just occurred.

I took a sweater from a drawer and laid it in the duffle with some underwear and socks. "Packing light," Rena said, watching me from the bed.

"I won't be gone that long," I told her. "We'll drive each other crazy, in a couple of weeks she'll throw me out and then I'll be home, no worse for wear." I zipped the bag and kissed Rena on the cheek. "Don't forget to feed the birds."

"I know," she said.

"And water the greenhouse, every day."

"I *know*," she said. I took one last look around my little house, walked the garden, loaded the car. It had more vegetables in it than anything else: squash, beets, potatoes for my dad.

"Maybe I should pee again," I said to Rena, making to

get out of the car.

"For godssake, Grace, just go already," she said. And so I did. I pulled down the road and it was just as I had feared: I was driving again, as if I had never lived in New Hope at all.

They say the angels take themselves lightly and so are able to fly. But I was no angel, pulling myself along the slush-clogged roads. I stopped only to pee and to fill the no-spill cup Rena had given me with coffee. Each stop I made I stood in front of a pay phone, shifting from foot to foot like I was guilty of something; but in the end I never did call, either the home I was leaving or the home for which I was bound. I guarded my last days alone like a wary dog, saying nothing, even to the attendants when I payed them for gas.

By the time I crossed the line into our county snow had begun to fall, edging familiar landmarks in a brilliant white. JESUS SAVES, ETERNITY WHERE. But even if he gathered us to him now with those hands too big for his body, drew my mother to his breast and breathed lightly in and out against her hair, she was, I supposed, beyond anyone's saving. Maybe even mine, though I still felt willing to try.

There were no tracks in the driveway when I pulled in, and when I looked back from the doorstep the snow had already begun to fill in mine.

The door was open; "Mom?" I called when I walked in.

"Up here," she called back, and I took off my shoes, following the trail of her voice.

We spent a lot of our time in the car that winter, driving the slippery roads back and forth between doctors and hospitals and home. She couldn't eat much after treatments though I made my mother great kettles of soup, cooking in the evenings when I felt she'd gone to sleep. I ate what I could of it and in a few days poured the rest down the sink, planning as I let the disposal run what I'd make the next day. Noodle soup, barley soup, some hopeless consommé .

I'd assumed she would be a more docile patient, as if sickness by its nature rasped one's edges smooth, but she was more herself than ever now, briefcase and cigarettes lying open on the bed. "Why are you doing that, you shouldn't be doing that," I said when I came upstairs my first day there and found her chain-smoking.

She had a Vogue magazine in her lap with a picture of a woman in an evening gown adrift on a white water raft. "I'm still your mother," she told me sharply, her eyes narrowed in warning like she'd punish me if I went on. Then she held the magazine up against her chest. "This is me, Grace," she said.

I brought my mother a cup of coffee and some toast on a tray. "Grace," she said, "for godssake, do something about your hair."

"Do something yourself," I snapped. But my mother didn't have any hair. Her hand went up and rested on the chiffon scarf she wore, her face gone red, then white when the weight of my words settled in. I put my hand on her forearm, warm where the sun fell.

"You *could* use a haircut," she said.

"How is she?" my sister said when she called each week. Our connection kept cutting in and out, and I came to expect our conversations to always be like this, making whole sense from only half her words.

"The same," I told her, "pretty much the same."

"I can't hear you!" she yelled, speaking in hurried Spanish to someone I couldn't hear on the line.

"Talk to her yourself," I said.

"Don't bother her," she told me, "I'd rather talk to you."

"She's awake," I said, yelling to my mother to pick up.

"God damn you Grace," my sister swore, "I told you I don't want to talk to her."

But when I put the receiver down I could hear my mother laughing on the line upstairs, and long silences during which she said little but sighed a lot. She asked for books about Nicaragua which I brought home for her from the library, and she read them all from cover to cover, taking small, infrequent sips from a glass of water and smoking her Camels to ash.

My father never rang the bell, he walked in the house as he had when he used to live there. It was a constant source of annoyance to my mother, though she accepted his visits now like the offerings they were meant to be: a kind of protracted apology, a show of loyalty couched in the layers of their conversation together, more like siblings than anything else.

"Does your *girlfriend* know you're here?" my mother would ask.

"You're still a bitch," my father would say, handing her the crossword puzzle he'd torn from the Chicago Sun Times.

I listened to them from outside the door. I remembered sitting on the milk box when they fought, praying that they stay together, no matter what. To me, clouds signified the presence of God, and if the sky were particularly dramatic that day all the better, God was on my side and angry, too. When my father moved away he took his things from the house a handful at a time: a couple of suits, a carton of books, some ties, records, a few shirts. He didn't ring the bell when he came, and for a minute I'd forget that he'd really gone away, a man home for lunch like all the other dads on our block.

"This is not your house!" my mother would scream, throwing balls of his own socks at him.

"Don't forget who's paying the mortgage!" he'd yell back, grab what he wanted and storm out.

"Don't cry, Gracie," he'd say when he came outside. "Everything's fine," he'd tell me, "you're good kids, I know that, you'll bounce right back from this, you'll see." But what I felt in my chest was more convincing than my father gently coaxing me to stop crying and go inside to my mother. I could not believe him then, and instead sat sniffling on the milk box, watching him drive away.

Now I sat with my father in the kitchen after his visits, drinking coffee and eating cinnamon toast. It was the house

I'd always wanted, the peaceful house, my parents caring for one another while I sat by and took their caring in. We never said much, and when one of my mother's friends dropped by it was the signal my father took to leave. He didn't like the way they looked at him, as if he were the cause for her being sick. But in two days or so he'd come back, barging in, little gifts like offerings in his hands.

When my mother could no longer wash herself she insisted we take her to the hospital.

"But I don't mind," I told her, trying to keep her in her bed. My brother had come home by then, and I hadn't gotten used to the long beard he wore, or the bulk he had gained, or his stunning eyes.

"Don't be difficult, Mother," he said.

"I'll not have the two of you treating me like a child," she warned us, pulling the collar of her housecoat closed.

"Then stop acting like one," my brother snapped back. He'd lost none of his fire the years he'd been away. He ran a youth center in Tel Aviv for Arabs and Jews, and the authoritarian tone he used on my mother was one clearly developed to keep thirteen-year-olds in check.

"I don't need this," my mother said. Her skin had fallen away from her cheeks in folds but her eyes stood out like amulets in her face. "Either help me or get out," she said. My brother fell back a bit as if her words had blown him there. He left the room and I followed, catching him before he slammed his door.

"It's what she wants," I said.

"She should be here, at home," he said, "it's our duty to take care of her."

"She doesn't want us to," I told him as gently as I could.

"*You* don't want to, isn't that it, Grace?" he said. He glared at me and shook his arm free.

"Think what you want," I told him, my voice gone flat. I turned and climbed the attic stairs and sat on the daybed shaking. In the same way he used to catch me as a child, seizing on the one grain of painful truth I felt and using it to sway me, of course my brother was right: I was tired of watching my mother waste away, I was afraid of having to touch her in ways I thought no child ever should. I longed to give her over to someone more capable of caring for her than me, someone whose job it was to remain calm, who didn't shrink from the weight of her failing body's needs. I hadn't slept much the whole time I'd been back and when I did my dreams were littered with her dying, her funeral, her burial, the flowers we'd place on her grave. So real they served only to enervate me, I woke each morning more restless and more numb, like a person who's drunk too much coffee at the wake.

I wanted to make a cup of tea for my mother. There was a field, and in the field grew the plants I was to harvest and brew: wake robin, cloistered heart, one-flowered cancer root. I clipped what I thought I needed and carried the plants to a sideboard outdoors on the porch. I boiled water in a copper pot and placed the plants in there one stem at a time. There were swallows' nests tucked under the eaves of the porch, and every so often a bird would swoop in low, knocking bits of straw and little stones into my pot. I tried to scoop the straw out with a spoon, but it looked like the other plants so I left it in there, worrying as I did that the tea had been ruined.

My mother lay beneath a quilt I'd made from silk neckties in all the colors of the sky. When the brew turned red I knew it was time for her to drink. I filled a ladle and carried it in to her, holding one hand beneath the bowl to catch drips. The tea was hot and it burned my hand, leaving one red mark for each drop of tea. When I reached her there were ten marks in the palm of my hand.

I fed my mother the tea and she closed her eyes. There was nothing I could do. She flew away.

My brother returned to his mysterious ways, disappearing after furtive conversations with old friends on the phone; and I took to my old ways as well, sitting for long hours with my mother in her room. "Go out and *do* something," she'd say, but I never felt like leaving. Even when her friends came by to sit on the end of her bed and chat, even then I knew my mother liked me to be there, so I stayed. As in a boat adrift on an easy bay, I was lulled into thinking things would always be this way, my mother anchored, finally, in the sea of her giant bed while I sailed around her, bringing soup, bringing tea.

True to her word, though, my mother decided she'd had enough one day and checked herself into the hospital, calling a taxi to come and pick her up in case someone made a fuss and tried to stop her from going.

"I can take care of you," I told her, weaving my fingers in the hem of her quilt, "aren't I taking care of you?"

"Look," she said, holding her hands out. They looked like the roots of a tree to me. "It's all downhill from here,

Grace," she said.

Although I couldn't bear to, I sent the cab away and drove her to the hospital myself. She let me bundle her into her otter coat, less because the day was cold than that she needed a cushion for her bones now, they all felt like elbows prodding her on when she sat.

My mother had grown suppurating wounds on her legs and feet, and she made me go out of the room when the nurses came to tend her, she did not want me to watch them pull the soiled bandages back, dab at her indignant body with their sponges and gloves, cover it unceremoniously up again. She continued to view her illness with that same detached surprise, but she could not reconcile herself to its attendant publicity: her first day in the hospital she had me hang a sign on her door that read Please Knock, and everyone, save my father, obeyed. Nor could she bear the hush that overcame people when they first walked in the door, as if sickness made the body more intolerant of the voice. For this reason she kept the television on, so that in order to be heard you had to speak in your full voice.

Once a day I'd go home and fill the old tub in my mother's bathroom with the hottest water I could stand. I'd ease myself in slowly and wait until I felt the blood pounding against my skin, then I'd turn the shower on full force and cry. I made an art of wailing in the tub, puffing my belly out, watching the water bead up on my slick, healthy breasts. I thought if I let myself do this now, that when my mother finally died I'd see her off silently, I'd just give in. But of course that wasn't how it was. I kept my fist in her sparse hair long after she passed, my brother and father urging, cajoling. "Let go, Grace," they said again and again.

But I wasn't holding on to my mother, she was holding on to me. The body had begun to smell bad the moment she died, as if her spirit had taken her good scent along with it when it went, and I could not stop the bile from rising in my stomach, sickening me more the longer I was held captive to her empty husk. I stayed there long after her scalp had cooled, and I swear I'd be there still if they hadn't gently pried me loose like a sleeping child's fingers held fast to a doll.

"Eve," my grandmother scolded, "let the girl be." And when my mother obeyed I was happy for a moment, happier than I ever remember being in my life. I let the men of my family pull me from the room and sit me in a chair while they went to make arrangements with the people in charge, and then I remembered that my mother was gone, and I began to weep for missing her, and why hadn't I known this before, I don't know, but I missed my mother as I have always missed her, she was my one original longing, elusive and substantial as the spinning earth.

We split the money but kept the house, none of us able to decide what to do. My sister wanted the china, my brother the maple dining set, but it was too costly to think of shipping the things, and besides, they reasoned, they'd eventually both be moving back. We could rent the place, we said, though we knew we never would. The thought of other people inhabiting our separate rooms was more than any of us could stand, it made us feel jealous and erased. The house was all paid for, and other than the taxes it cost little to maintain. And so it was decided we would keep the place, leaving my siblings satisfied and relieved that it would still be here, unchanged, when they came home.

Everyone assumed I'd go back West, but I never did. Rena, my friends, the profligate plum trees and the garden I'd made, I missed them all, but I just couldn't bring myself to get in the car and drive away again. I had Rena put my stuff in someone's garage and as far as I know it's all still there, rusted and moldy and longing for use.

I spent my first nights alone in the attic listening to the house sleep, straining my ears for the sounds of my grandmother's raspy breathing, my father's snore, my brother's furtive window, my sister laughing, sneaking out at night, my mother's slippered feet. I prayed for a ghost but one never appeared, and in a week or so I knew I couldn't live there anymore. It was way too full of its own emptiness, that old house of ours. Even if I'd wanted to, I could not, by myself, fill it up.

I took my inheritance money and bought this place, five acres and an old house I stripped and painted white when I moved in. Once a fragment of some thousands of acres, it was owned by a farmer who gave this piece to his youngest daughter as a gift on the day she left home. So furious at the slight (her brothers making off with the rest of the operation) she put her share on the market and never talked to her dad again. She wouldn't sell to her brothers and no one else seemed to want it, too small to do anything with and smack in the center of a family dispute. It cost forty thousand then but it's worth half that now, its value waning steadily as the moon, though when it will wax again not a soul can say.

Moving in didn't take very long. I brought only the

necessities from my mother's house, which in my life didn't amount to much: blankets, a skillet, some hangers for my clothes. I swept and scrubbed the floors, cleaned the windows, washed the stove. When I was finished I couldn't bring myself to sit still yet; I made a circuit through all the rooms and ended up standing in the empty hall, hands hung latent as wind chimes at my sides. It was late, I was tired, but I remembered one thing I could do. My grandmother had kept a special *mezuzah* on her door, and I took it now from my handbag and unwrapped it from a wad of paper towels. I used my shoe as a hammer and hung it in the doorframe. It looked inky green and old in the light. I touched the *mezuzah* as she had each time entering and exiting her room, I kissed my fingertips lightly like her, though faith never did well up in my breast like the cloud of steam I imagined it to be. *If I ever needed you, now's the time,* I thought to myself, trying to feel her touch there. But I didn't smell her scent in the air, nor hear her voice whispering what next for me to do.

I pressed my head against the screen door, the night chill in my face. The moon made a filtered pattern on the clean wood floor, an owl grazed the trees with its wings. I don't know how long I stood there like that, but in time I had to go to sleep. And sleep I did, for the first time since my return, dreamless and restful as a stone.

The place was overgrown but I didn't mind. I rented a tiller to turn some ground, and the second season here I bought my own. I made friends with the people who run the co-op in town, bought some chickens, built a greenhouse, ran a stall at the market in summer. I don't earn much cash but my payments are low, and as far as I'm concerned I own a fortune in soil: friable to the elbow, black and worthy as oil.

The women nearby were friendly and the men polite. I met Mennonite and Amish folks who appreciated what I was trying to do, a flea amid giants in an oversized land, and they told me where to get organic seed and fabrics for my quilts. It took some time to set up house, picking through yard sales to find the useful things I like: a woodstove, a bed frame, a table and chairs. When I was finished the place felt like home, and I've never regretted having stayed. I made long-distance calls to my friends out West, and to Rena, who had moved back East while I'd been away. I made weekly forays to the library in town, absorbing myself in novels and gardening books until another week went by. I thought of my mother often and talked to my siblings on the phone once a month, and before my father left I had supper every week at his house. We ate the chili he made or chicken of Lavonne's, and I looked forward to the company though tired soon of listening to them argue over the TV. Often I left there with a headache, glad for the silence of my own house. I didn't ever invite them to come out here but sometimes, on Sundays, my father came driving up the road unannounced. We'd sit those days looking out at the sky, sipping coffee or eating a piece of fruit.

"You have a nice life here," he'd say to me, "I envy your being alone," patting me lightly on the leg. "I just don't feel equal to it," he said to me with admiring eyes, returning to his lively house.

"Neither do I," I said, but that didn't stop my father from going on home. I looked at his face, and for the first time I recognized my inheritance there, the way his chin was cast slightly upward and away, as if what was most interesting to him lay somewhere only he could see.

I picked Mr. Yoder and Lydia up and drove us into town. "I want your opinion on something," I told them, and they didn't press me on what.

"I trust it's on a subject I know something about," was all Mr. Yoder said as he climbed into the truck. It was cool and getting colder and clouds had begun to gather in the northwestern sky. I tapped my fingers nervously on the wheel as I drove, and Lydia told a story about her neighbor who'd just gone blind. "Mad?" she was saying, "I'll say he was mad. Threw dishes against a wall all day, until his wife gave him the broom and told him he didn't need the use of his eyes to sweep up." Lydia wore a flowered jacket and yellow slacks, and I imagined how sad it would be to miss seeing her like that, so easy in her roomy clothes, foot up on the dash as she talked.

I parked the truck in front of my mother's house; I took the key from my bag and let us in.

"If you're thinking of moving, don't," Mr. Yoder said. He was seventy and stern and this was the nearest thing to outward affection I'd heard come out of his mouth.

"Thanks for saying it, but I'm not," I told him.

"But this is your home," Lydia said as soon as we walked in the door.

"It's been some years," I said.

I walked across the living room and raised the slatted blinds. A determined spring sun passed through, and for the first time I could see how sad the place looked, as if not being lived in was harder on it than all the years of our serious wear had ever been.

We walked through the house slowly not saying much, and then I took them to the Hamburg Inn for a cup of coffee and some pie. We crowded into a booth and ordered.

"What do you want from us, Grace?" Mr. Yoder said.

"I don't know," I lied.

"Sell it," Lydia told me, stirring sugar into her cup.

Mr. Yoder twisted his feed cap slightly in his hands. "Once it's gone you can't ever get it back," he said. The two of them stared at each other across the table.

The pie came and we passed the plates out: peach for Mr. Yoder, banana for Lydia, rhubarb for me. I took a bite and it was just the way I liked it, equally sour and sweet on my tongue.

"It's not just my decision," I said by way of explanation. "I have a sister and a brother, and even though he doesn't own it I feel like my dad should have a say in this, too."

My friends looked up from their plates, surprised. "I assumed he was dead," Lydia told me. "I thought you were alone."

They didn't press me for the story though suddenly I knew I owed it to them both to tell.

Mr. Yoder laid his fork beside his plate. He cleared his throat. "If they haven't said by now then they're waiting on you, Grace," he said. "Whatever you decide, they'll do."

"I'm not so sure about that," I told him.

"It's not about them," Lydia said.

We finished our pie and they let me pay. It was late March and a heavy cloud spit sleet across the road, making it difficult to see the way. The wipers made their rhythmic sweep across the glass, and the three of us sat lulled by them into an easy silence that seemed to mark our day. Sleet or no, I could drive that road, even blind as Lydia's neighbor, entering into a kind of symbiosis with the wheel that pulled me away from the family's old house and on in the direction of my home.

I went over to my mother's house and sat at the piano, grazing my fingers back and forth along the keys. I went up into the attic for a bit, but I felt finished with the past right then, and only grew wheezy from the dust. A realtor came and met me there, and I took her on a tour of the place, from my grandmother's bedroom on the ground floor, through the kitchen, up the stairs.

"And why are you selling now?" she asked me, notepad in hand, ready to write down what I had to say.

"It just feels like time," is what I said.

The world is vast and varied but its tools are not: a spade for digging, a pail with which to haul water. Ancestors visit my body when I turn potatoes from the ground, and if I grew rice in Indonesia it would be the same, the blood of the people who eat inhabiting the food we grow: cultivating lichens in the Arctic with its short, bright sun, on the tundra, the desert with its frenzied bursts of rain, watching the cactus bloom from some aged promise, nothing. I am sitting near this window as I have each March for a few years now, pinching seedlings, watching the evergreens reach for their share of light. In my hand a cup of tea and in my lap a plan for what I'm making, with my body, this season. Faith for the farmer resides not as much in her heart as in her knees. As for methods, my neighbors and I will disagree, they with their ammonia and their herbicides, me with my manure teas, my cover crops of buckwheat and clover. But we will do this work and do this work, making what we can from what we have as one constructs a garden for and out of oneself, or a memory, or a greening life.

This world is grown up from a diaspora of seeds, scattered and sown by the restless birds. And so my family is scattered as well, rare weeds taking root in distant soils: my sister to the south, my brother to the west, my father to the east and down, spending his long days golfing beneath a reliable sun. It occurs to me now that I have been living as a bowl for us all, holding our memories as one holds a finger in a book to hold the place, and I have held our place, and mowed its lawn, and dusted its objects when I had the time to spare.

I worked outside today, turning the compost with a fork, standing back to watch the steam rise up, satisfied with the season's slow boil. Toward the bottom of the pile I found a squash seed growing, despite the dark down there, pushing its way upward and clear of its hull. I stood looking out at the weather as it tumbled fast at me across the plains. Well below the several feet of topsoil I could feel the axis, around which we've turned all our lives, turning too, toward some inexorable future I seemed to have forgotten until now. *Begin, begin*, I heard it sing, and was it the spring weather making me hear this song, or had I simply run through my cache of the past, with nothing left to do but move on? I thrust my fork into the pile, letting the seedling land where it may. They call these renegades *volunteers*, but I'm not sure what choice any of us have. It will, or it will not, show itself in my garden this year, snaking its way through my freshly mulched beans, getting itself grown no matter what. Later, when its leaves are gone, I'll take that plant's bastard fruit and make something from it, I'm sure I will, some sweetly steaming pie of possibility to eat.